BU

By Kat

Katy xo

Other books by Karli Perrin

April Showers (April #1)

April Fools (April #2)

The Honey Trap

Short stories –

The Gift

The Book Boyfriend

The Book Addict

Dedication

To Roxy.

Thank you for having the patience of a saint. This one is for you.

Author's note - Although Buzz can be read as a standalone, it is advised to read The Honey Trap first as it provides some background to Buzz and Lori's story.

The Honey Trap is currently enrolled in Kindle Unlimited.

"This isn't the story of how we met.

This is the story of how I lost her.

And how I tried to win her back."

- Buzz

PART ONE

CHAPTER ONE

Thursday.

My favorite day of the week.

I get to finish work early, the weekend is within touching distance and last but definitely not least; it's Throwback Thursday, motherfuckers. It's the one day of the week where I get to sleep with my exes, no strings attached. It even has its own hashtag on social media. People mistakenly use it to post pictures from the past, but I know the real meaning behind it.

I unlock my phone and scroll down my long list of contacts, considering all of my options.

Amber – out of town.

Brittany – has a boyfriend.

Ellie – too clingy.

Hailee – married.

Lacey – pregnant.

Marissa – talks too much.

Rebecca – likes to cuddle.

Stacey – psychopath.

Victoria – works on Thursdays.

Decisions, decisions.

I sigh and tap the call button next to Stacey's name. She always answers on the sixth ring. When we started dating, if you can even call it that, she answered immediately. It was like she was constantly waiting for me to call. After one month, she would wait one ring before answering. After two months, she waited two rings. We made it to six rings before I ended it. That was over a year ago, but she still acts like it was yesterday. She's bitter and badmouths me to all of her friends but that still doesn't stop them from trying to hook up with me.

She answers on the sixth ring. Even though she's a psycho, she's a predictable one. I know exactly what I'm getting with her. Angry hate sex and if she's in a good mood, a blowjob. "What do you want?"

"It's nice to talk to you, too," I reply sarcastically.

She sighs. "I'm busy. What do you want?"

"Busy doing what?"

"Quit with the small talk, Buzz. Why are you calling me? Do you want to fuck?"

I laugh. *This* is why I chose to call Stacey. Straight down to business. "Well if you're offering..."

"I know that's the only reason you've called me, douchebag. Give me an hour. I need to get rid of Gary."

"Who's Gary?"

"The new guy. I'm training him up."

"Training him up? At work?" The last time I bothered to listen, she was still working at Sephora.

"No. I've been seeing him for a few weeks but he can't give me an orgasm. He's really funny and kind so I don't want to give up on him just yet."

I chuckle. "He's not *that* kind if he can't even give you an orgasm but he's already made me laugh so I see what you mean about him being funny."

2

She hangs up.

"See. It's easy," I tell Stacey as she stops shuddering after having her second orgasm of the night. I only usually give her the one but tonight I'm trying to prove a point. "Gary must be broken."

She sits up and scowls. "Why do you always have to ruin the moment?"

"Hey, you should be thanking me."

"Thanking you for what? Using me?" She looks around for her panties.

"I'm only using you as much as you're using me. I can get my orgasms wherever I want but apparently you can't."

She catches the thong that I throw at her. "You're such an asshole. This won't be happening again."

"Okay."

"I mean it."

"I'll see you next week."

She narrows her eyes as she buttons up her shirt. "Everything was going great between us. Why did you have to go and ruin it? We could have been happy together."

I shudder at the thought of being in a relationship with her. It was never going great. I've never wanted a girlfriend. I only agreed to it to shut her up. I was super busy at work and the thought of regular sex appealed to me. Plus, she wasn't such a psychopath until the end.

"Stacey, we've been through this at least fifty times. You faked being pregnant. Everything was *not* going great."

"I only did that to get your attention. To get your love."

"Well it did the opposite, didn't it?" I've never loved her. I never even came close. I did the right thing by breaking up with her. It was a kind move on my part. She wanted love and commitment and I would never have been able to give her either of those things. Now she's free to settle down with Mr Nice Guy Gary. It's called *settling* down for a reason and that's something I'll never do.

"This won't be happening again," she says again, as though she's trying to convince herself.

"Then you better hope Gary's a quick learner."

"You're such a smug bastard."

"It was lovely to see you, Stacey."

"Shame I can't say the same thing in return." She shakes her head. "At least Gary respects women."

"Oh, are we talking about respect now? I lost all *respect* for you when you photoshopped your name onto somebody else's baby scan then cut all the sleeves off my shirts when I found out you were lying."

She walks over to the door. "I'm glad I did that. I hope it taught you a lesson." *It did. It taught me that you're batshit crazy.* "You spend way too much money on material things."

Says the girl who refuses to step foot in Target. "I can spend my hard-earned cash on whatever the fuck I want." I wave her away. "Don't let the door hit you on the way out."

Lucky escape, I think to myself as I hear it close behind her. I walk over to the window, just to check that she's actually left. It wouldn't surprise me if she pretended to leave so she could kill me in my sleep. I watch as she unlocks her car and just as she's about to climb in, she looks up and gives me the middle finger. I chuckle and blow her a kiss.

Five minutes later, I call Marissa.

CHAPTER TWO

I skip into my boss's office the next morning feeling refreshed which is good considering I only had four hours sleep. "TGIF," I announce as I close the door behind me. I freeze when I get my first look at him. "Woah, what happened to you?" He didn't get laid, that's for sure. "You look like shit." Luckily, my boss is also my best friend.

"Thanks. You really know how to make a person feel good, don't you?"

I grin. "Oh, believe me, I do. In fact, I made Stacey feel *very* good last night."

"Psycho ex-girlfriend Stacey?"

"Correct."

"I thought you said you'd rather cut off your balls with a blunt knife than ever see her again? And that you'd rather be celibate for the rest of your life than..."

"Bro!" I shout, interrupting him. "Don't use the C word." How dare he speak about celibacy in my presence. He knows that's my number one fear. I even applied to be on the TV show *Fear Factor* but apparently they don't class it as a genuine fear. But cotton wool is? Pricks.

Mason laughs. "I thought you two were over for good this time."

"We are but it was Thursday yesterday."

"What's that got to do with anything?"

He never listens to me. I've mentioned it to him hundreds of times but in his defense, he's been busy dealing with his *own* psycho ex the past few months.

"Throwback Thursday. I'm allowed to sleep with my exes, no strings attached."

"I'm seriously contemplating firing you for saying that."

"Why? It's a real thing. Just like today is Follow Friday." I draw a hash tag in the air. "Or what I like to call hash tag FF."

He pretends to hit his head against the desk. "Please tell me you didn't just do that."

"As I was saying, Follow Friday is where I allow a hot girl to follow me home."

"Oh, so you're going to *allow* them to go home with you rather than spending hours *persuading* them?"

"Yep, you'll see exactly how it works tonight. Are we still on for drinks?"

"Yeah but only if you stop being lame."

"I will if you will. Anyway, how did it go last night? Is that why you look so rough?" Surely meeting up with his soon-to-be ex-wife and some of her friends who still don't know about their separation would have that affect.

"Again, thank you. But yeah, it was bad."

"Do you wanna talk about it?"

"Not really."

"Good, I'm not in the mood to listen to you whine today."

"Remind me, why are we friends again?" He hands me a piece of paper. "Here, go and make yourself useful."

"What's this?"

"A phone number."

I roll my eyes. "I can see that, Einstein, but whose? Is it your assistant's? Has she finally fallen for my good looks and boyish charm?" I doubt it. She hates me ever since I kissed her at last year's Christmas party. Don't worry, it had nothing to do with my kissing ability. I'm golden in that area. It was because she found me fondling Kirsty from accounting ten minutes later. It's not my fault that her mom didn't teach her how to share.

He ignores me. "I want you to trace it and find out as much as you can."

I try to look as serious as possible. "The last time you asked me to do this, somebody wound up dead."

"What the hell are you talking about?"

I laugh. I love playing around with him. He's too damn serious most of the time. It's only going to get worse as he goes through the divorce. "Sorry, I couldn't resist. I've been watching too much Netflix recently."

"Just trace the number."

"Okay but a little more information would be nice."

"I met somebody last night."

"What do you mean you *met somebody*?" I gasp. "A woman?"

He shrugs. "It's no big deal."

"So then why are you asking me to trace her number?"

"I'm not. I'm asking you to trace her friend's number."

"You're making no sense. Why have you got her friend's number?"

"Because the woman I met used my phone to call her friend."

A huge grin breaks out across my face. "Dude, why was she using your phone? You fucked her, didn't you?"

"She borrowed my phone at the restaurant. Nothing else happened."

"Liar. At least now I know the real reason why you look like shit."

He points to the door. "Just trace the damn number, Buzz."

I skip out of the room. It looks like I might be getting the real Mason back.

I hesitate for about half a second before pressing the call button. Why the hell would I waste an hour of my life hacking into systems and triangulating signals when I could just call the damn number?

Just when I think it's about to go to voicemail, somebody picks up. "Hello?"

I sit up a little straighter. "Hello. Who am I speaking to?"

"Who am *I* speaking to?" I imagine her with crossed arms and narrowed eyes.

I'm probably going to get sacked for what I'm about to do but that's never stopped me before. "This is Mason Hunter."

I'm almost positive I hear a little gasp but when she replies, her voice is cool and composed. "What can I do for you, Mr Hunter?" Cool, composed and *shit hot.* Breathy, husky, seductive. I could listen to it all day…and night. I don't usually like it when women talk during sex, unless they're screaming my name of course, but for her, I'd make an exception.

"Please call me Mason."

"What can I do for you, Mason?"

Nothing for him. But you can do a lot for me. *To* me. "I met a woman yesterday at Scoma's. She used my cell to call this number. Are you her friend? Her roommate?"

"Maybe. Maybe not."

I raise my eyebrow. Why is she being so secretive? The air of mystery is making her even hotter. I love a good chase. I'm not used to it seeing as though women can't help but throw themselves at me. "I'm just trying to find her, that's all. Can you help?"

"Why are you trying to find her?"

I have no fucking idea why Mason is trying to find her. To fuck her, hopefully. He seriously needs to get laid. He's been celibate for the last six months. *Six months.* Half a fucking year. I'm surprised his dick hasn't shriveled up. Hey, maybe it has. It would explain why he's such a grumpy bastard these days. "I want to invite her out for drinks." Okay, now I'm *definitely* going to get sacked.

"When?" she asks, her interest clearly piqued.

"Um, tonight." *Shit.* Goodbye job. Goodbye best friend.

"Where? What time?"

"Pulse. Seven thirty."

"I'll pass the message on."

"You should come too," I tell her. "I'm bringing a friend. He's a great guy. The *best* guy. You'll like him."

She laughs and it turns my dick to stone in mere seconds. Well, well, well, it looks like I've found myself a dick whisperer, Ladies and Gentlemen. I haven't even seen what she looks like but apparently I'm the owner of a non-judgmental penis. Who knew?

"I can decide for myself," she replies, her voice laced with amusement.

"So that means you're coming?" *She will be once I get her in my bed. Over and over and…*

"Maybe," she replies, breaking my train of thought.

"I'll see you at seven thirty." I laugh when she hangs up. It takes me about a minute to recover. It takes my dick much longer.

I think I might have found my match.

CHAPTER THREE

"Do you want the good news or the bad news?" I ask Mason when we finish eating our lunch.

"Bad first," he replies.

"I traced the number, but I couldn't get a name or address because it's a pay as you go sim card."

"So what's the good news?"

Here goes nothing. "Well I could have triangulated the signal, but I decided to save time and just dial the number instead. The good news is that she sounds really fucking hot. Thanks for helping a brother out, I've saved her number for my own personal use."

He groans. "You called it?"

"Yep. She's got this husky voice thing going on, she could make a shit ton of money working for one of those sex chat lines." I'd call her every damn day.

He places his head in his hands. "Why? Why would you do that? I could have just called her if I knew that's what you were going to do."

"Yeah you could have but you didn't."

"For fuck sake, Buzz. I asked you to trace the number not call it."

"You also asked me to find out as much information as possible which is what I was trying to do. What's the problem?"

He sighs. "The problem is that you never follow instructions. Just tell me what you know. Did she mention her friend?"

"Yeah, it's her roommate." *I think.*

"I thought so. Last night she said something about feeding their dog. Did you get an address or anything?"

"Let me think about that for a second...oh yeah, she told me her address after giving me her social security number and bank details." I chuckle. "I didn't ask for her address. That would have been weird, even for me." I put on my best creepy voice. "Do you like scary movies? What are you wearing?"

"Fuck you. What else did you find out?"

"Nothing. She wouldn't tell me anything, not even her name. It was like talking to the secret service."

"So let me get this straight, you called the number even though I didn't ask you to and the only thing you found out was that they're roommates?"

I'm not even sure about that. "Correct."

"Well thanks for being so helpful."

"You're welcome," I reply.

"Did you mention me?"

"The world doesn't revolve around you, boss."

"Answer the question."

I shrug. "No. I didn't *mention* you."

He groans. "Oh no, what did you do?"

"If I tell you, you're not allowed to fire me. I was only trying to help."

"Just tell me."

I try not to wince. "I may or may not have pretended to be you."

He closes his eyes and takes a deep breath. "Get out."

"Aww come on, it's not that bad. I thought there was more chance of her telling me something if she believed I was you."

"Well clearly it didn't work, did it?"

I shrug. "I didn't anticipate her being so guarded. Chicks before dicks and all that crap."

"Just get out. Go somewhere far away and stay there for a while."

"Awesome, does that mean I can work from home this afternoon?"

"No. Now get out before I come over there and kick your ass."

"You couldn't kick my..." I dart out of the room when he stands up. Even though I joke about him being precious, he works out like a beast and I wouldn't want to push him too far. Which is what I'm probably about to do. I stick my head around the door. "Um, there's one more thing you should know. I've invited them to come for drinks with us tonight."

CHAPTER FOUR

Please Lord, let her be hot.

I scan the club, hoping my dick will seek her out and lead me to her.

And after about ten minutes, it does. *The world's greatest wingman.* I'm walking over to the bar to find Mason when I stop dead in my tracks. I don't believe in fate or any of that bullshit but when her bright green eyes lock with mine, I know that I've found her. It's as though an invisible thread is pulling me to her. "You're here to see me," I announce as her hungry eyes look me up and down. *Talk.* Let me hear that husky little voice of yours. Prove that I'm right.

"Are you sure about that?" she asks.

Thank the fucking lord. "I'm sure." I hold my hand out. "Buzz."

"Excuse me?"

"My name."

"Your name is Buzz?" I nod. "That's unusual."

"There's a story behind it."

"Which is?"

I let my arm fall to my side. "You haven't even told me your name yet."

"Lori." She glances at the pretty blonde standing next to her. "And this is Sophia."

"Nice to meet you both."

"Are you here alone?"

15

"No. I'm with my friend."

She looks around the room. "Your invisible friend?"

I chuckle. "Nah, I haven't seen him since I was about seven. My *real* friend is over at the bar."

"Wait," she says, tilting her head to one side. "Have we met before? Your voice sounds familiar."

Uh oh. She's supposed to believe that it was Mason who called her, not me. I peruse every inch of her perfect body. Her killer curves will be the death of me. "Trust me, if we had met before, you'd damn well remember it."

She doesn't look convinced. Any other day, I would love to be all alone with two beautiful women but I'm relieved when I spot Mason over Lori's shoulder. They both turn around when I motion for him to join us. "Are you just going to stand there?" I shout to him when he doesn't move. He's looking at Sophia, all gooey-eyed. Could he be any more obvious? *Loser.*

"Ladies, this is my friend, Mason," I tell them when he finally remembers how his legs work. "Mason, meet my new friends, Lori and Sophia."

"I'm Lori and this is Sophia," Lori clarifies.

"Hello," Mason replies, concentrating only on Sophia.

"The ladies were keeping me company seeing as though you ditched me," I tell him.

Lori laughs. "You're a big boy, I'm sure you can be left alone for ten minutes."

"You're right," I reply. "I am a big boy. *Very* big."

"Yeah, what are you, about six foot four?" she asks.

I wink. "I wasn't talking about my height, sweetheart."

"I know, I was joking. Just like you were joking about being big, *sweetheart*."

I raise an eyebrow, excited by her willingness to play along. "How do you know I was joking if you've never seen it? Maybe you should take a look so you can set the record straight."

She shrugs. "I would but I've left my microscope at home."

I try to keep a straight face as Mason and Sophia walk away from us. "Well maybe we should go and get it right now. I'll help you find it."

"Find what? The microscope or your penis? Does it usually take two people?"

I can't hide my grin any longer. "Where did you come from?" She's like a different fucking species.

"I'm not telling you where I live, creep."

I shrug. "I guess I'll see for myself later."

"You're not coming home with me."

"Not yet."

"Not *ever*. Are you always like this?"

"Sexy and charming? Yes." I sigh. "It's exhausting."

"*You're* exhausting."

"You ain't seen nothing yet, sweetheart."

"And I intend on keeping it that way."

It's cute how naïve she is. It won't last very long. "I could make you fall in love with me tonight if I really wanted to," I say, sitting down on the sofa next to us.

"Oh, you could, could you?"

"Yep but lucky for you, I like the chase."

She rolls her eyes. "I'm *so* lucky." I sit back and wait. Any second now she's going to take the bait. Any seco... "So how would you make me fall in love with you then?"

Bingo. "I'm not sure you could handle it."

"Stop flattering yourself and just tell me. Your lines don't work on me."

"Fine. Are you sure you want to do this? Once you fall for me, there's no going back."

She sits down opposite me. "I'm sure."

"If you could invite anyone in the world to dinner who would it be?"

She frowns. "What's that got to do with anything?"

"Just answer the question."

"Channing Tatum."

"Are you being serious? You could invite *anyone* but you're going to choose Channing Tatum?"

"Yep. He's divorced now. Is this your little party trick? Because if you can get me a dinner date with

Channing, I would probably fall for you. Although Channing would have first dibs."

I chuckle. "First dibs?" She nods. "And if he's not interested in what you're offering, then you're all mine?"

"Sure."

That's good to know. If all else fails, I know an agent who could probably put me in touch with him. "Would you like to be famous?"

"No, I would hate that. I like having my own privacy. What about you?"

"I'm kind of a big deal already."

"Okay, Mr Big Shot."

"Oh, I like how that sounds coming out of your mouth." My dick twitches. "Call me Mr Big Shot again. Actually, try Mr *Huge* Shot."

She raises an eyebrow. "No, pervert."

"Before you call someone, do you rehearse what you're going to say?"

"I thought you were making me fall in love with you..."

"I am. Just roll with it."

She shrugs. "I hate making phone calls. I avoid them at all costs. My preferred method of communication goes like this - Facebook, Instagram, Twitter, text messages, e-mail, carrier pigeon, message in a bottle, *phone call*."

I laugh. "I love your voice. I'd call you every night if I could."

"Please don't do that."

"Why do you hate it so much?"

"I don't know. I think it's because people expect a response right away. I can't stop and think about what I'm going to say or think of an excuse. I prefer to type a message then edit it five hundred times first. We're far too advanced for telephone calls now. They should be banned."

"Oh yeah, they're a danger to humanity. You'll be saying we're too advanced for face-to-face conversations next."

She weighs it up. "Well…I do try to avoid people as much as I can."

"That's a lie or you wouldn't be here."

"I'm only here because I can't get a signal which means nobody can call me."

I grin. "What makes a perfect day for you?"

"Staying in bed all day…"

"Deal," I interrupt. "Let's do it. How about tomorrow?"

"How about no?"

"No doesn't work for me."

She rolls her eyes. "As I was saying before you rudely interrupted me…staying in bed all day *reading*."

I groan. "*Reading*."

"Yes, *reading*. It's where you open a book and read the words until you reach the last page. You might have heard of it."

"No. You'll have to show me tomorrow."

"You're persistent, aren't you? Is that how you're going to make me fall in love with you? Nag me until I give in just to shut you up?"

"No but that's a good plan B. So what else? Reading and…"

"Nothing. I'd only move to get food and to pee. I'm a fast reader so I could probably fit three or four books in." She sighs happily.

"Well if I was there, I could bring food to you so you would only need to get up to pee."

"Or I could just order take-out and Sophia could bring it to my bed."

"There's no need to bother Sophia."

She raises an eyebrow. "There's no need to bother *me* but you're still doing it anyway."

"When did you last sing?"

"You mean in the shower or…"

I rest my chin on my hands. "Yes. Tell me about the last time you sang in the shower. Paint me a beautiful picture." I close my eyes but open them when she throws a pillow at my head. What kind of club has pillows? "Hey! You brought showering up, not me."

"I sing a lot. I sing when I'm cooking or cleaning or yeah, in the shower."

"Serenade me."

"Um, no. That's not going to happen. I'd need a few drinks before I sing to you."

I pretend to stand up. "I'll go and get the drinks. Seriously though, I know this awesome little karaoke bar."

"And are *you* going to serenade *me?*"

"Of course. I'll serenade you whenever you want, sweetheart."

"Go on then. Do it right now."

I stand up and begin to lift my t-shirt up while singing, "*It's getting hot in here, so take off all your clothes…*"

"I told you to sing, not strip. Please put your clothes back on." She clasps her hands together and looks up at the ceiling.

I chuckle. "Are you praying?"

"No. Why would I be praying?" She turns to face me but closes her eyes. "Seriously. Put your t-shirt back on." She can't help herself and sneakily opens one eye. "Lord, help me."

I wink at a group of giggling women walking by. "Don't you like what you see? Okay, now you're definitely praying."

She blushes. "Fine. I'm praying that you put your damn shirt back on."

I reluctantly cover up. "What did you think of my singing?"

"Singing? I don't remember any singing."

I sigh. "There's more to me than just great abs, you know." I look down at my crotch. "I also have a great di…"

"Next question," she shouts.

I sit back down. "If you lived until you were ninety and could choose to keep the mind or body of a thirty year old, which one would you choose?"

"Mind, without a doubt. All those wonderful memories. What about you? I suppose you'd want to keep your perfect abs and...*other things*."

"My dick will always be perfect, even when I'm ninety."

She leans in and whispers. "You may not be able to get it up when you're that old."

"As long as you're around, I'll always be able to get it up."

"This is the weirdest conversation I've ever had."

"How do you think you're going to die?"

"Anddd it just got even weirder. What's the deal with all these questions? I feel like I'm speed dating or something."

I raise my eyebrow. "Oh, we're on a date? Then you should know that I never go past third base on first dates. I hope that's not a problem."

"We both know that this isn't a date so why would that ever be a problem?"

"It's a problem because once you have a little taste of me, you'll want the whole damn thing. You'll be begging for more and I'll have to say no. I have morals, you know."

She sighs. "To answer your question, at the rate this interrogation is going, I'll probably die in this club. I won't be able to survive on alcohol and potato chips for longer than a few days."

"Why not? That's what I survived on in college. You'll be fine."

"How do *you* think you're going to die?"

"During sex, probably."

She rolls her eyes. "When you're ninety?"

"You'll be there to see how old I am."

She puts on an old lady voice. "He always said he was going to die during sex. Thank god he gave me one last mind-blowing orgasm."

I chuckle. "Hell yeah, I did. Can I have that written on my tombstone?"

"Yeah if you don't care about your great grandchildren reading it."

"*Our* great grandchildren will appreciate the fact that I kept you satisfied."

"Next question."

"Name three things you think we have in common."

"I've got nothing."

"Oh, come on!"

"I guess we both breathe the same air."

"Well, opposites attract," I tell her. "Remember that."

"Next."

"What are you most grateful for?"

She looks over at Sophia who is laughing at something Mason just said. "Sophia. She's my family now."

I nod. "I know the feeling. Mason is like a brother to me." My heart sinks when I remember that he's my *only* brother these days. "He has helped me through some really shitty times."

Her eyes soften. "Like what?"

I shrug. "I don't want to kill the mood."

"You won't. I want to know more about you."

"My brother died a few years ago."

"I'm so sorry," she says.

"My mom and dad broke up when I was young, so my older brother was like a father to me. I took it really hard. Mason stepped up. I joke that he's like a dad to me but I really look up to him. He steers me in the right direction." I wink, trying to lighten the mood. "He steered me here tonight. He steered me to *you*."

"I'm glad he did."

We stare at each other for what feels like minutes. "Are you in love with me yet?"

She swallows hard. "Not yet."

"I guess I better keep going then. If you could change anything about the way you were raised, what would it be?"

"Hmmmm." She takes a moment to think about it. "I wish that I was taught how to be confident and realize my self-worth. It took me a really long time to love myself."

"But you're beautiful. I can't believe you've struggled with confidence issues."

"I guess we all have our own issues. Well, I'm sure *you* don't but…"

"No, I do."

"Really? What are they?"

I run a hand across my jaw. "Are we really doing this? Are we going deep?"

"Isn't that what you enjoy?" I raise an eyebrow and she raises one right back. "Going deep?"

"I guess you'll find out." She looks away when the intensity gets too much. "People have always tried to change me," I tell her. "It makes me feel like I'm not good enough. Like I can't be the real me."

"Is that why you're always joking around?"

"I guess I sometimes use humor as a shield. If I project this larger than life version of myself then it won't hurt as much when people don't want me."

Her eyes turn sad. "Who wouldn't want *you*?"

"A lot of people."

"A lot of *stupid* people."

"Keep going," I joke.

"I'm not going to massage your ego anymore."

"Will you massage something else instead?"

She throws the other pillow at me. "Now what am I supposed to throw at you?"

"Yourself?"

"You don't have to put up a shield around me, you know. You don't have to joke about everything."

"I wasn't joking. I'd love it if you threw yourself at me." I smile. "But seriously, I'm not putting up a shield around you. I'm being myself. Anyway, enough about me. Tell me more about you. Tell me about your life."

"Oh, um, I've had a pretty boring life. There's not much to tell. I was born and raised here in San Francisco. Brought up by my mom. We travelled around quite a lot. I was always the nerdy one at school. I've always loved to read."

"Boyfriends?"

She looks down at her feet and shrugs. "Two serious ones."

"What happened?"

"They weren't right for me. We wanted different things."

"They had *you*, what more could they want?"

"Sweet talker."

"No, I'm being serious. What did they want that you didn't?"

"Well my last boyfriend wanted to fuck other women so there's that..."

"Fuck him. Not literally. Don't do that. He doesn't deserve you."

"You can say that again."

"He doesn't deserve you."

She smiles. "Are you going to tell me what all this is about?"

"Soon. Is there something that you've dreamed about doing for a long time?"

"Opening my own bookshop. There would be giant beanbags and cake and it would be amazing."

"So why haven't you done it?"

"Because I can't afford it. I spend all of my money on books."

I laugh. "What's your greatest accomplishment?"

"Besides meeting you?"

"Obviously."

"Making my own money. Not needing to rely on anybody else."

"It feels good, doesn't it?"

"*So* good."

I wiggle my eyebrows up and down. "You know what else feels good?"

She looks around for more pillows. "Are there more questions or are you done?"

"What is your most treasured memory?"

"My first book signing. I was *so* excited. The coffee didn't help. I made a complete idiot of myself in front of Colleen Hoover. She's my unicorn author."

"Your what?"

"Unicorn. My favorite of all time, basically."

"And what about your most terrible memory?"

"Isn't that obvious? Making an idiot of myself in front of Colleen freaking Hoover. I was talking way too fast and ended up spitting my chewing gum out." I burst out laughing. "No, don't laugh! It landed on her hand!"

"I would probably die of embarrassment."

"Right? And then the second time I met her, I almost killed her. I gave her some sweets and about five minutes later, she started choking on one of them."

"Why did you do that?" I ask with a serious face now. "She won't be able to write any more books if you kill her."

"Well I obviously didn't mean to."

"She's probably going to write you into one of her books as a psychopath."

"I wouldn't care. I'd love to be a character in one of her books."

"Even if she killed you in it?"

"I still wouldn't care."

"What if *you* killed one of her other characters?"

She gasps. "No way! I wouldn't!"

"Who's your favorite character of hers?"

"That's a tough one. Probably Will Cooper."

"Maybe you'll give Will Cooper some sweets and he chokes and dies."

"This definitely isn't going to make me fall in love with you..."

I laugh. "We'll see about that. Speaking of death, if you knew you only had one year to live, would you live your life differently?"

"Oh great, the morbid questions are back. I'd probably quit my job and go travelling but I'm pretty happy with my life. What about you?"

"I'd have more sex."

"You mean you don't get enough?"

I sigh dramatically. "Not nearly enough."

"Poor you. Let me get my violin out."

"I hope violin is code for something else."

"Pass me the pillows so I can throw them at your head again."

I grab them and sit on top of them. "If you want them, you'll have to come and get them."

"Or I could just find something else to throw at you instead."

"Name something you like about me."

"You're very forward, aren't you?"

"Good answer."

"That wasn't my answer. Although I do find it refreshing. I like that you make me laugh. I like that you're honest. I like that you actually seem interested in what I'm saying." She shrugs. "I like your face."

I'm grinning like an idiot. "You sure do like a lot of things about me, huh?"

"Your turn. What do you like about me?"

"Everything so far." I wink. "You're my unicorn."

She laughs. "Okay, sweet talker. Next question."

"Finish this sentence. I wish I had someone with whom I could…"

"Laugh with. Cry with. Share my life with."

"And what about - Buzz has a huge…"

"Ego."

I chuckle. "Is there anything I should know about you? Anything about your life?"

She frowns and sits up a little straighter. "Like what?"

"Anything. We might as well be honest with each other from the start."

"I've only known you for five minutes. You know more than enough." She seems a little rattled which makes me want to dig deeper but now isn't the right time.

"When was the last time you cried?"

"That's easy. Last night."

"Over what?"

"I had a premonition that I was going to meet you."

"And you cried tears of joy," I shoot back.

"You wish. I cried over A Court of Wings and Ruin."

"A Court of what?"

"It's a book. I was re-reading it for like the tenth time."

"Why do you re-read a book? Surely once you've read it, you don't need to read it again. You already know everything that happens."

"Why do you re-watch the same movies or play the same games? Why do you go on more than one date with the same person? Some books were meant to be read over and over again."

"I think I can guess the answer to this one. If your house was to catch fire, which item would you save?"

"My books."

"How many do you own?"

"Hundreds. Three, maybe four."

"*Four hundred?* I fucking hope your house doesn't catch fire. All that paper. Owning all those books is probably a fire hazard in itself."

"That's a risk I'm willing to take."

"Okay, we have one last thing to do." I pat the couch next to me. "Come and sit down over here."

"Why?"

"You need to look into my eyes for one whole minute."

"Why? Are you going to hypnotize me?"

"Just trust me."

She sighs and sits down beside me. "This is so weird."

"Ready?"

"I guess so."

"Sixty seconds starts now."

I tune out everything else around us and concentrate on nothing but her. It feels like I've known her for a long time which is a little unsettling. I'm used to undressing women with my eyes but this is different. This is real. I've never felt so vulnerable and it's scary but also exhilarating. After what feels like hours, *days*, she clears her throat. "Um, I think it's been longer than a minute."

It definitely has. "I don't think so."

She laughs but refuses to look away. "Are you going to tell me what all of this is about?"

"I read an article in the New York Times a couple of years ago. It was about how two strangers can fall in love by answering thirty six questions."

She blushes. "I didn't think you actually meant it when you said you could make me fall in love with you."

"Oh, I meant it."

"So you've just asked me thirty six questions?"

"No. A lot of them are very similar."

"How the hell do you remember so many questions? That is seriously impressive but also extremely worrying."

I chuckle. "I have a photographic memory. It's one of my many talents. Do you want me to show you what else I'm good at?"

"Remember this - *no*."

I lean back and grin. "Don't worry, I'm remembering everything about this moment. Every tiny detail."

"Why?"

"Because I want to remember the night you first started falling for me."

"Is that right?"

"Yep."

"How many other women have you done this with?"

"None."

We're both silent as she tries to judge whether I'm telling the truth. "And the creepy staring thing?"

"Just you."

"Well I'm flattered." She finally tears her eyes away from mine and I take a deep breath. It feels like my lungs have been starved of oxygen for the past few minutes. She stands up and smooths down her dress. "At least now you know that it doesn't work. You don't have to waste your time doing it with anybody else."

"Aww, that's cute."

"What is?"

"The fact that you don't want me to do it with anybody else. You don't want them to fall in love with me too."

"*Too?*"

I shrug. "Hey, if it was in the New York Times then it must be true, right? The media never lies. Just go with it. Stop trying to fight it."

"There's nothing to fight."

"Give it another month, Unicorn."

CHAPTER FIVE

One month later

"This is one of my favorites," she says before gently kissing my tattoo.

I look down at the little flame which says, 'raise hell' underneath it. "Why?" I ask.

"Because it's perfect for you."

I chuckle. "Thanks, I think."

She nods. "You're unashamedly you. You're the most authentic person I've ever met. You're honest and passionate and you *always* get what you want. You raise hell and boy do you own it."

I smile lovingly at her. "Well now it's one of my favorites too."

"You mean it wasn't already?"

I can feel my walls coming up thick and fast but for her, I knock them down. *Only for her.* "No, it wasn't. It takes me back to a dark time. I got it just after my brother died. He always used to say it to me when we were growing up." I shrug. "It's bittersweet. It's a reminder of what I had but also a reminder of what I've lost."

She leans up and kisses me. "And there's me thinking that you just walked into a tattoo shop and picked the first one you saw."

She always knows how to lighten the mood and for that, I'm truly thankful. She's the light to my dark. The calm to my storm. I laugh. "Nah, I'm very careful when it comes to choosing tattoos. I can't say the same for women. I walked into the club that night and you were the first woman I laid eyes on. Mason should feel very lucky that I didn't spot Sophia first."

She scowls but quickly forgets why when I pull her on top of me. "And now," I say, lifting my hips up. "We raise hell."

The next day, I show up at her house unannounced. "Trick or treat?" I ask when she opens the door.

Her jaw drops. "What the hell are you doing?" she asks, eyeing my costume.

"What do you mean? It's Halloween."

"I didn't think I was seeing you until tomorrow. I thought you were working."

I raise one eyebrow. "Oh, believe me, I'm going to work you *so* fucking hard."

I love it when she blushes. "What are you wearing?"

"You seriously don't know?" I step backwards and spin around.

"Of course I know. I just…I can't…it's a lot to take in right now." She strokes one of my wings. "Where did you even get them? They look exactly how I've always imagined them."

And so they should. I've spent the past few days reading and researching the book that she mentioned on the night we first met and paid a Victoria's Secret costume designer over two thousand dollars to make me some wings. I know it's crazy but she's worth it. "Be careful," I tell her. "You know what happens if you stroke Illyrian wings."

She gasps. "Wait…did you…no…but how would you know…"

I chuckle. "You're having a conversation with yourself. Spit it out."

"Did you *read the book*?"

"A Court of Mist and Fury? Of course I read it. The second book was much better than the first, in my opinion."

"Oh my god, I love you," she blurts out. Her eyes go wide when she realizes what she just said.

We stare at each other for a long moment until a shit-eating grin takes over my entire face. "I told you to give it another month. Now, are you going to invite me inside? I'm ready for my treat."

CHAPTER SIX

"What's in the bag?" Lori asks as we walk down the street, hand in hand.

"It's a surprise."

"Another one? First you surprise me by cooking me breakfast and now you're taking me on a surprise date."

"You're skipping the most important part of our morning."

"Which time?" she asks.

"I enjoyed them all equally. Although I *really* enjoyed taking a shower with you." I wink at her and we carry on walking until we reach the coffee shop.

She looks up at the sign. "*Sanctum*. Is this where you're taking me or are we getting coffee?"

I push the door open and a little bell chimes. "Both." She smiles as I hold the door open for her. Most of the women I know would be disappointed by a date at a coffee shop, but Lori is different. She's *special*. I've brought her here for a reason and I watch her carefully, waiting to see her reaction.

She gasps when she spots the giant, two-seater beanbags and floor to ceiling bookshelves. "Oh. My. Freaking. God! What *is* this place?"

"I remembered that your dream is to open a bookshop with beanbags and cake."

"And it already exists!" she says, looking around the room.

"Not quite. They don't sell books here, but customers can stay for as long as they'd like and read any of the books in here." I point to the counter. "And look; there's cake."

"I've died and gone to heaven. Can I just live here?"

I chuckle. "I knew you'd like it."

"I don't like it; I love it! I can't believe I'm only just finding out about this place." She walks over to one of the bookshelves and leans her head to one side as she peruses the titles.

"I wasn't sure if they would have any of the genres you like so I brought back-up."

"Are you joking? They have thousands of books in here."

I take off my backpack and she turns around when I begin to unzip it. "I looked on your Goodreads and came prepared."

She peeks inside the bag and then squeals. "You did not!"

"I did."

"You bought them for me?"

"Yep."

"You could have just picked one!"

"I couldn't choose. They all sounded good."

"You read the freaking blurbs?"

"Of course I did. I was tempted to keep one of them for myself. I need to find out what happens when

40

April falls for her teacher." I raise my eyebrow. "You have a thing for forbidden romance, huh?"

The way she looks at me with so much intensity makes my heart race. "What did I ever do to deserve you?"

"I keep asking myself the same thing."

She stands on her tiptoes and kisses my neck before whispering, "Tonight is all about you. We can do anything you want."

"Anything?"

"Anything."

I pull her closer to me. "My plan has worked."

She kisses me before taking the backpack from me. "That's still hours away. What are you going to do all afternoon?"

"What do you mean? I'm going to be right here with you, eating cake and drinking coffee."

"Okay but you should know that when I read, there's no talking allowed."

I chuckle. "That's fine. I'll take a nap. I need to make sure I'm fully rested for later. I'm going to put all of your damn book boyfriends to shame."

CHAPTER SEVEN

When something seems too good to be true, it's because it usually is. So when Lori sits me down a couple of weeks later and tells me that we need to talk, I mentally prepare myself for bad news. "What's up?" I ask.

"I've been keeping something from you."

My stomach drops. "What do you mean?"

"I'm sorry, Buzz. I've been lying to you and I'm ashamed that I've let it go on for so long. I should have been honest with you from the start but I never thought you would stick around long enough for this to be an issue."

"Just tell me, Lori."

"I'm not a nurse. I don't work shifts."

I frown. "So what *do* you do?"

"I'm a honey trapper."

"A what?"

"I trap cheating men. I get hired by their wives and girlfriends."

"How do you trap them?"

"I mostly flirt with them. I wear a microphone, so their partners receive a recording of them planning to come home with me. But sometimes…well, sometimes I have to kiss them."

My heart starts to beat a little faster. Okay, *a lot* faster. "Why?"

"Because I need to prove they're willing to cheat. I have an undercover photographer with me who captures it all."

I feel sick to my stomach. "Doesn't the recording prove they're willing to cheat?"

"Some women believe that planning to cheat and actually going through with it are two different things."

"So what happens after you kiss?"

"I go home. I usually sneak out of the back and they're completely unaware of what just happened."

"So you don't confront them?"

"No. That wouldn't be safe."

"None of it sounds safe." I take a deep breath and rub at my temples. "So let me get this straight…you don't call or text them? There's no prior relationship? You just turn up, see if they're willing to kiss you and then leave?"

"Most of the time, yes." She sighs. "But sometimes we have to drive with them to a rented apartment."

I stand up. "What the fuck?"

"If it's a full trap, I have to try and prove that they're prepared to take it one step further. I need to show that they're willing to get into a car with me and drive to my fake apartment. Their partners are usually waiting inside to confront them. We have security there too."

"I thought you said it was safe."

"It is. I leave immediately and the guy who drives us there is also part of the security team. They pretend to be cab drivers. I'm never completely alone with the men. I get paid a lot of money, but I wouldn't do the job if it was unsafe."

"And what happens when they want to get revenge? What if they try to find you?"

She shrugs. "I wear a wig and use a fake name. I usually drive further out to avoid bumping into the guys that I trap. I haven't had to deal with anything like that yet."

"*Yet.*"

"I'm so sorry that I lied to you. It's been eating me up inside."

"If you were honest with me from the start, it wouldn't have been an issue."

"It wouldn't?"

"No. But I have a problem with the lying."

"I know. I've messed up."

"I need some time to process it all." This is why I don't do relationships. I let myself be open and vulnerable for the first time in, well, *forever*, and this is what happens. "I'll call you," I tell her as I go to leave.

"I hope I haven't lost you," she says as I walk away.

I pause but don't look back. I don't tell her that it only hurts this much because she's the one who *found* me.

CHAPTER EIGHT

"Do you want cookie dough or mint choc chip?" I ask, taking two spoons out of the drawer.

"Cookie dough, obviously," Lori replies.

I walk over to her with a grin on my face. "That's why we're perfect for each other. I want the mint choc chip."

"Of course you do. Why do you think I bought it?"

I place a hand over my heart. "You bought it just for me?"

"Yeah. You owe me."

"Oh, I'll repay the favor, don't you worry about that. I can repay you right now if you want me to." I sit down next to her and pull her onto my lap. "I'll repay you all night long." Her phone rings just as I lean in to kiss her. "Ignore it," I say before placing my lips on hers. She groans and pulls away. "Lor, seriously. Just ignore it and get back here."

"I can't. It's my work cell."

I sigh. "And?" It's been six weeks since I found out about her job and I'm still coming to terms with it. Even though I always want her to be honest with me, I think I preferred it when I was oblivious. *What you don't know can't hurt you.* And it hurts me when I think about her with other men. It hurts me when her damn cell keeps interrupting our date nights. I don't care if it's the busiest time of the year for honey trapping. I don't care that she catches the most cheaters at Christmas parties. The only thing I care about is her. *Us.*

"And you know I can't ignore it," she replies.

"Yes, you can. Nobody's going to die. It's not like you're some kind of surgeon on call."

She scowls. "I may not be a surgeon, but I still take my career seriously. When the phone rings, I answer it."

"Stop being defensive."

"I'm not."

"There you go again." I groan and adjust the contents of my boxer shorts as she answers the call. I open the ice cream and dig in as I watch her. "Can somebody else do it?" she asks her boss. "No, it's fine. What time?" She pauses. "Okay, send me the information."

She hangs up and I pull the spoon out of my mouth. "Let me guess; you're leaving me?"

"I'm sorry. I should be back in a couple of hours. I asked if somebody else could go but it's a high-profile case; some reality star. She doesn't trust any of the newer girls to trap him."

"Another douchebag from Big Brother?"

She looks down at her feet. "No. Survivor."

I shake my head as I place the lid back on to the ice cream. "Well, so much for Netflix and chill."

"Are you going to wait here for me?"

"Nah, I need a drink." *A stiff one.* "I'll call around and see who is free."

"I'm sorry."

I walk past her, carrying both tubs of ice cream. "Me too."

"Please don't be pissed at me."

"I'm not. I'm pissed at your job. I'm pissed at your boss." I don't know why I'm even feeling this way. It shouldn't surprise me anymore. Since she came clean about her job, she's been working a lot more. I can't remember the last time we spent the whole evening together. This time last year, it wouldn't bother me one bit. In fact, it would be the perfect relationship. Lots of sex and not much conversation. No dates. No sleepovers. But Lori makes me want more and right now, I'm not getting that.

She walks over to me and snuggles into my chest. "I'll call you when I'm done. Maybe you can come back later."

"Maybe."

I already know that I won't be back.

"I just don't get why we can't stay in one place," Mason says as we walk into the fourth bar of the night. "The drinks are all the same."

"I get bored easily."

"Well, I already know that."

"Then why are you even asking? I like to people watch." And I've also been secretly looking out for Lori. I know she's at a bar but I don't know which one. I check my cell and have no missed calls which means she can't be home yet. I look around the room as we walk over to the bar but there's no sign of her.

"Are you ready to talk about it?" Mason asks as I lean against the counter.

"Nope."

"I'm here for you, Brother. I went through the same thing with Sophia, so I know how it feels."

"Nah. Soph quit as soon as you two got together. She wanted to be with you more than she wanted the job. Lori obviously thinks what we have isn't worth saving."

"I don't believe that for one second. Have you spoken to her about it?"

"Kind of. Not properly. I told her to ignore her cell earlier but she wouldn't listen. She knows I don't like what she does but she does it anyway." Mason says something in response, but I don't make out any of the words. No, all I hear is Lori's laugh. I look around the room once more and that's when I see her. She's sitting in a booth in the far corner and some dickhead has his arm around her. He's whispering into her ear and she's got her hand on his knee. They look like a couple. A *real* couple. I can feel the rage stirring deep inside of me. I start to walk over to them but a hand pulls me back. "Stop," Mason says firmly. "Don't be stupid."

I spin around to face him. "Don't call me stupid." He might be my best friend but I'm fucking raging right now.

"Then stop acting stupid. It's not real."

"It looks pretty fucking real to me. Her hand is on his leg. Why the fuck is she touching him?"

"It's her job."

"No. Her job is to trap him. To catch *him* touching *her* leg, not the other way around."

"It's just an act."

"Then she deserves a fucking Oscar."

Mason sighs and wraps an arm around my neck. "You don't need to watch this. Let's go home and in about an hour, Lori will come home to you. Nobody else. *You.*"

"The way she's looking at him right now, it wouldn't surprise me if she went home with him instead."

"She's good at her job."

"A little *too* good if you ask me. I'm going over there."

"You'll lose her if you do that. Let's just go to a different bar. We can meet her when she's done."

"No. I'm staying here."

"Okay well at least sit down." He pulls up a chair and I do as he says. "Listen, Brother. You know that I love you, but you had the choice to end it when you found out and you decided not to. You chose to stay with her."

"I'm aware of what happened."

"Then you can't throw it in her face." I know that he's right but I don't want to admit it. We sit in silence for a few minutes. "I really think you need to be honest with her. Keeping it bottled up is just going to make everything ten times worse."

I shrug. "It's my shit, not hers. I'll take care of it."

"A relationship is a two-way street. She needs to know how you're feeling."

"I'll take care of it," I say again, a little blunter this time. I order another drink and down it in one as soon as it arrives.

After ten minutes of pure hell and a whole load of self-control, Mason finally convinces me to leave. I stand up and look over at them one last time and that's when the world comes to a shuddering halt.

They're kissing.

I stand there, frozen to the spot, and wait for it to end.

But it doesn't.

A few seconds later, his mouth is still on hers.

Why isn't she stopping? Why isn't she pulling away? She's proved that he's a cheater so now it's game over.

STOP KISSING HIM.

I see red when his hand touches her ass. I turn around and swipe at the empty glasses on the counter, causing them to fall to the ground and smash.

Mason quickly grabs hold of me and drags me away, pushing me out of a fire door. "Please calm down," he says, sounding worried.

He should be.

"Let me back in there."

I'm bigger than him and if I really wanted to, I could get past him. But I don't want to fight Mason and I don't particularly want to fight the loser she was kissing. I just want him to back the fuck away from my girl. I shout, letting some of my anger out. Mason gets right up in my face and makes me look at him. "You can get through this. Come back to my place and we can talk about it. We can figure out what to do."

"I already know what I need to do."

I'm just struggling to accept it.

CHAPTER NINE

"What time do you want to catch the movie tomorrow?" I ask Lori as I scroll through my phone. "There's a show at eight fifteen and another at nine thirty. We could grab food first then go to the nine thirty show."

"Tomorrow? I can't. I'm working."

I sigh. "Since when?"

"Yesterday."

"Do you not remember us making plans? Obviously not."

"I'm sorry. We can go on Saturday instead."

"I want to go tomorrow."

"Then ask Mason."

I close my eyes and count to ten. This past week has been super difficult. Ever since I saw her in the bar, I've been doubting everything. I've tried my hardest to forget about it but I'm struggling. "I don't want to go with Mason. I want to go with you. Can't your boss send somebody else instead? You work way too much."

She frowns. "Buzz, you work from seven in the morning until seven in the evening."

"Exactly. That's why I want to see you afterwards but you're always working."

"Well yeah, it's part of my job. I work evenings. We hardly get any jobs to trap people in the day. Most people are at work."

"Yes, because they have normal jobs."

She folds her arms across her chest. "Don't be an ass about it."

"I'm not being an ass. I think I've been very patient and understanding so far."

"*So far.* Do you have a problem? I feel like you're not saying something."

I consider lying to her. I consider brushing it under the carpet like I have done for the past week. For the past month. But I can't. It's eating me up inside. I'm starting to resent her and I won't allow it. She doesn't deserve that. I stand up and slide my cell into my jeans pocket. "I can't do this anymore."

"Do what?"

I gesture between us. "This. Us. I need some time to figure things out."

She swallows hard. "I don't…why…is it because of my job?"

"That's a huge part of it, yeah."

"But I thought you accepted it."

"I did. I do. But I don't like it. I don't like how it makes me feel. I don't like what it's doing to us."

"And how does it make you feel?"

"Like I'm losing my fucking mind. I don't want you around other men."

"Why didn't you tell me any of this when I first told you?"

"Because I thought I'd be okay with it, but it turns out I'm not. I'm not okay with being priority number two."

"Priority number two?" She throws her hands up in the air. "Stop being so childish."

"I'm being *honest*. I don't think I'm ready."

"Ready for what exactly?"

"All of it. All of these feelings."

"You mean you're not ready to love me?"

I'm pretty sure I wouldn't be feeling this way if I wasn't falling in love with her. I wouldn't care about her job. I wouldn't care about the other men. "I never wanted a girlfriend…"

"So then why did you make me one?" she interrupts. "Why did you string me along if you knew you didn't want this?"

"I thought I did. I just need some time. I'm not used to feeling this way."

"So you're scared?"

"Of course I am. I'm scared of fucking everything up."

"But that's what you're doing anyway by running away."

"I'm not running away."

"Yes, you are! When are you going to grow up? When are you going to accept that this is the best you're going to get?"

"I already know that."

"Then why are you pushing me away?"

"Because you deserve better."

"Oh my god!" she shouts. "Don't you dare come out with that bullshit! Don't tell me what I deserve. I *know* what I deserve. I *know* what I want. Don't try and put this on me. You're the one ending it for your own stupid, selfish reasons. You're not doing this for me. You're doing it for yourself."

"That's not true. I'm doing it for both of us." I sigh. "I can't handle…" I'm about to tell her about the other night and about the sleepless nights which followed when she interrupts me again.

"You can't handle a relationship? You can't handle all these big boy emotions? What are you going to do instead, Buzz? Are you going to carry on fucking everything with a pulse? Are you going to be a player for the rest of your life?"

"No. I don't want that at all."

I follow her as she walks over to the front door. "You obviously do."

"Lori, I don't. I just need some time. I promise I'm going to…"

She holds up her hand. "I don't want any more of your promises. Get out of my house. I'll collect any of your things and give them to Sophia. She can pass them to Mason."

"Please can we just talk for a little longer?"

"No. I've heard everything I need to hear. We're done." Her eyes fill with tears as she opens the door. "I don't even know why I'm mad at you. This is my own fault. I thought I could change you. I should have followed my head instead of my stupid heart."

"Lor, you *have* changed me."

She opens the door even wider. "You wouldn't be leaving right now if I had."

"That's exactly *why* I'm leaving. I'm trying to do the right thing. I'm trying to figure this out but it's all new to me and you don't deserve to be a guinea pig. I want to do better. I want to *be* better."

"Well Lord knows *I'll* be better off without you messing up my life."

She closes the door in my face and the only thing stopping my heart from shattering is knowing that this can't be the end for us.

It can't be.

Can it?

Her departing words haunt me for the next six months.

PART TWO

CHAPTER TEN

I can't believe my best friend has turned into a 'we' man. I loosen my tie in an attempt to hide my disgust. Don't get me wrong, *I'm* happy that *he's* happy but I hate hearing couples refer to themselves as 'we' all of the time. I was looking forward to a nice cold beer after a long day at the office but no, they have plans…*again*. It wouldn't surprise me if Sophia holds his dick while he's taking a piss.

Loved up motherfuckers.

"Sex plans or actual plans?" I ask.

He laughs. "In my world, sex plans *are* actual plans."

"You know what I mean, dumbass. Are you ditching me just to get laid?"

"No. We have dinner plans."

I pretend to yawn but it turns into a genuine one. "Let me guess; romantic dinner for two?"

His steps falter. "Um, no. No…we're actually having a couple of guests over to the new house. Sophia's been talking about hosting a dinner party for a while now." He winks. "She's doing all of the cooking so if I'm off sick tomorrow, you know why."

It's blatantly obvious that he's trying to change the subject. "Who are your guests, Mason?"

"Jeez, you're asking a lot of questions tonight."

"And you keep trying to dodge them. Just tell me. Will Lori be there? Is that why you're acting weird?" He nods and I try my best to act casual. "So where's my invite?"

"Sophia's super excited about hosting. We spent five hours shopping for dinner plates the other day. *Five*. For *plates*."

"And she's worried that I won't like the ones you chose?"

"No. I just don't want there to be any…awkwardness."

"Why would it be awkward? We're all adults. I'm sure we're both mature enough to eat dinner in the same room."

"*She* is."

"Sit me at the other end of your ridiculously oversized table if you're worried," I reply with a wink. "It's so big that I won't even be able to see her."

"Nah, I don't think it's a good idea."

"It's a great idea. I'll get to see how your new game room is coming along."

"Dude, she won't be alone."

I stop walking as his words hit me right in the gut. "Oh."

"Yeah. Sorry I didn't mention it. I didn't want to upset you but that's no excuse. I should have told you."

"Why would it upset me? I'm the one who broke up with her, remember?" We continue walking in silence for a couple of minutes until my head feels like it's about to explode. The question pours out of me before I can even try to stop it. "Who is he?"

He sighs. "I don't know."

"Who is he?" I ask again.

"I honestly don't know. I haven't heard Sophia talk about him much."

"You haven't heard her talk about him *much*. So what *have* you heard?"

"Just little snippets here and there, places he was taking her and that kind of thing. This is why I didn't mention anything to you; because I don't know how serious it is and I knew you'd act like this."

"Act like what?"

"Like *this*."

I pick at an invisible piece of thread on my jacket. "What time?"

"How about you come to the next one instead?"

"What time?" I say again.

He stops walking and turns to me, placing his hands on my shoulders. "You know that I love you, Brother, but if you ruin this for Sophia then you're fired. I mean it."

I grin as I mock salute him. "Yes, boss."

"Please don't make me regret this. Seven thirty. Bring flowers."

CHAPTER ELEVEN

I give myself a little pep talk as I pace up and down outside Mason's house.

It's going to be fine; it's just dinner.

With my ex.

Who I still think about every day.

And her new boyfriend.

Who I want to kill.

Stop it. I can do this. I *need* to do this. Maybe this will be the closure that we need. The closure that *I* need. Maybe seeing her happy with another man will allow me to finally move on.

I take a deep breath and ring the doorbell. We were friends once, we can be friends again.

Fuck that. Who am I kidding? We were never friends. What we had was way more than friendship. This is going to be a fucking disaster. I haven't seen her in six months, since the night we ended things…and it didn't end well. I didn't get any relief. I didn't get any closure. I got *heartache*.

If I was a better person, I would turn around and go home. If I was Mason, I would apologize and *then* go home. But I'm a selfish, masochistic prick who is probably going to be unemployed come tomorrow.

Mason opens the door and laughs. "Surely you could have found a tighter shirt to wear."

I look down at my denim shirt. It's not tight, it's just fitted. Okay, maybe it *is* a little tight. "Fuck you," I reply as I look him up and down. "Surely *you* could have changed out of your work clothes."

"I did."

"Well I can't tell. You look like you're about to go into a meeting."

"Maybe I am. Maybe it's about the banning of offensively tight t-shirts. Try buying an adult size next time."

He laughs as I push past him. "Hey, if you're about to have a meeting, does that mean I get to keep Sophia entertained?" Judging by the look on his face, we're done playing. "Is Lori here?" I ask as I glance around.

"Yes. Best behavior, remember?"

"Like always." I gesture to the flowers in my hand. "Where's Sophia?"

"Oh, you actually listened to me for once." He points to the end of the hallway. "She's in the kitchen cooking up a storm. Why did you buy her two bouquets? Kiss ass."

"I haven't. One's for Lori."

He raises an eyebrow. "Don't be a dick."

"What?" I feign innocence as I begin to walk backwards. "So I'm allowed to buy Sophia flowers but not Lori?"

"Correct. Sophia is the host. Lori is…well…Lori is somebody else's girlfriend." I try not to flinch as I turn my back to him. "Wait. That came out wrong..." I ignore him and carry on walking.

62

"Something smells delicious," I announce as I enter the kitchen.

Sophia looks up from her recipe book and smiles. "I hope it tastes equally as delicious."

"I'm sure it will."

"Well if it doesn't, you should know that I'm counting on you to eat all of it and make the others feel guilty for leaving theirs."

I laugh. "I've got your back, Soph. Why do you think I'm here? It sure as shit isn't to see Mason. I see enough of him at work."

She smiles but it turns sad. "Are you sure you're going to be okay tonight?"

"Of course I am." I wink. "I'm a big boy, remember? Thanks for letting me be the fifth wheel."

"You're always welcome here, Buzz. I think it'll be good for both of you to see each other moving on." She looks down at her engagement ring. I'm surprised it doesn't blind her. "We're going to be in each other's lives for a very long time so we need to make it work somehow. These past few months have been tough on all of us. I miss the good old days when we all used to hang out."

I nod. "Me too."

"You know I've always been on your team but Lori is my best friend. Please don't say or do anything to upset her."

"I'll try not to." I pause, trying to decide if I even want to know the answer to my next question. "Is she happy? You know…with him?"

"I'll let you be the judge of that," she replies after some careful consideration. So that's either a big fat no or she's head over heels in love with the guy. Please Lord, let it be the first.

I hand over the flowers. "These are for you."

She grins and leans in to take a sniff. "And there's me thinking that you'd bought them for Mason." She opens a cupboard and pulls out a glass vase. "Thank you."

"Well I guess I should go and wait with the other guests, huh?"

"You can stay in here and help me plate up if you'd prefer."

"Nah, they'll be getting bored without me. I'm the life and soul of the party."

"I won't be too much longer now. I just need to make sure that everything is properly cooked so I don't poison anyone."

"Hmmm, it wouldn't be too much of a shame if Lori's date got poisoned."

"Come on now, play nicely."

I laugh as I walk out of the room. "If I do anything to piss you off, just remember the pretty flowers that I got for you."

I head towards the game room and stop outside when I hear Mason talking to somebody else about his new poker table. For some reason, I carry on walking towards the lounge as though there's some kind of invisible thread pulling me.

And then I find out why.

I stop walking when I see her. I'm pretty sure I stop breathing too.

She's standing by the huge floor-to-ceiling windows, looking out at the world below. And she's wearing the dress. *The* dress. My favorite piece of clothing of all time. I mean, I always preferred her naked but if she *had* to wear something, I would always choose the green and black dress. The lace up back meant it was a fucking puzzle to get on but it took less than a second to get it off. My eyes fall to her strappy, fuck-me heels and I become insanely jealous and territorial. I feel like pulling my pants down and pissing all over her. Hey, it wouldn't be the first time I've done it. I swallow hard. I've been thinking about this moment for the past six months. Dreaming about it. First, she jumps into my arms and tells me how much she's missed me and then we have lots of sweaty make-up sex.

As if she senses me and my dirty thoughts, she glances over her shoulder and then does a double take. Our eyes meet and the whole world stops. In this moment, nothing else matters. Nothing else exists. You know in movies where a character is about to die and their whole life flashes before their eyes? Well that's how I feel right now. I'm seeing our whole relationship flash before me. The entire history of us. And this feeling that I have in my stomach, and in my throat, and in my heart…it feels like I'm the character in the film. I feel like I'm suffocating. Not being able to go to her, not being able to touch her…it's killing me.

This is a bad idea. I can already tell that I'm probably going to ruin Sophia's night which makes me feel shitty as she's been so kind to me. I should probably leave, or at least try to. I begin to walk backwards, watching her carefully, waiting for her to stop me. But she doesn't. Somebody else does. I spin around when we collide. The first thing I see is hair gel. Way too much hair gel. And then I see the whitest teeth that have ever existed. He's even more overdressed than Mason, which I didn't think was possible. I'm not sure why I didn't get the memo telling me to dress like I'm going to a funeral but judging by the way I'm feeling right now, maybe they're here for mine.

We size each other up; no longer men but predators. Luckily, I'm bigger than him in every way and higher up in the food chain. "Hey, man," he says as his eyes dart between me and Lori, probably wondering why the air is so thick with tension. I simply nod at him and watch as he walks over to her. "Hey, babe," he says before leaning in to give her a kiss on the lips. Just as I'm seriously contemplating pushing him through a window, she turns her head, forcing him to kiss her on the cheek instead. *That's my girl.* Only...she's not. Not anymore. And that's highlighted by the fact that some asshole has got his arm wrapped around her, clinging on to her as though she's about to disappear into thin air. But she hasn't looked at him once. Her eyes haven't left mine since the second she noticed me and for the first time in six months, I feel alive. This right here...this feeling, *this* is why I can't move on.

I sense Mason next to me but he doesn't say anything. Nobody does. We're all standing in complete silence. Me staring at her. All three of them staring at me. But then she makes her move. She forces a smile as her attention turns to Mason. "Well this is a surprise," she says, her gravelly voice almost giving me a boner.

Fuck, I miss her.

"You didn't mention that we were expecting more guests, Mason."

He clears his throat. "I...um...sorry...you...I'm just going to check on Sophia." He practically runs out of the room. *Pussy.*

66

I smile at how much my presence still affects her. "Good evening, Lori."

"Buzz," she replies through gritted teeth. "What are you doing here?"

I take a few steps closer to her. "It's nice to see you too."

"Have you brought a date?" she blurts out, looking disappointed in herself for asking.

"No. I'm not dating." I feel like dancing when her face floods with relief. She's always been super easy to read. I used to call her my little open book which she loved because she's such a huge book lover. But then our own story ended abruptly and now I have to listen to somebody calling her 'babe'. *Shoot me now.*

I walk over to her and hold out the flowers. "These are for you."

She frowns. "You bought me flowers?"

The new guy chuckles. "You bought my girlfriend flowers? Wow, now I feel like a massive idiot for not buying her any."

That's because you are one. I ignore him and gesture for her to take them. "I got your favorites."

He laughs. "Wait, who are you again?" *Who am I? Who the fuck are you?* "Are you here just to make me look bad?" *No, you do that all by yourself.* He taps the side of his head. "Sunflowers. I'll have to remember that."

Sophia comes rushing into the room with Mason close behind her. "Dinner time!" she shouts overenthusiastically. "Please come and sit down. Come,

come, come!" She practically drags me over to the table on the other side of the room.

Lori glares at Sophia. "I thought it was just the four of us this evening."

"So did I," she replies sweetly. "But Buzz is welcome here any time," she adds, nodding to me.

I smile. "Thanks, Soph."

I turn my attention to the prick who is currently helping Lori into her chair. I roll my eyes at such an old fashioned gesture and think back to a conversation I had with her where she told me that she hates men who insist on opening doors and paying for meals. What is she even doing with a guy like him? He already seems like the opposite to me in every way. Maybe I've just answered my own question.

I sit down opposite Lori, ignoring the little place card in front of me which has Sophia's name written on it. She rolls her eyes which makes me chuckle. "Something in your eye, Lori?"

"Nope," she simply replies.

"Then you better be careful. You know what happens to girls who won't stop rolling their eyes."

Hers go wide now, unable to play it cool at the mention of books. "Been watching the latest *Fifty Shades of Grey* movie, have you?"

"Nah," I reply. "I just remember that part from when I read it at your place that one time when I couldn't sleep. Remember, the next morning I was really horn…"

"Let me take your flowers," Sophia interrupts. "I'll go and put them in some water."

"I'll help you bring the dinner out," Mason tells her.

"No!" she protests, giving him a pointed look. "You stay here."

The new guy shuffles even closer to Lori and laces his fingers through hers.

I can't bear to look. "Where are the drinks at?" I ask Mason.

"Um, Sophia's matched the wine to the food."

"What a great idea," New guy says.

I ignore him and groan. "Please don't turn into one of *those*."

"One of those?" Mason asks with a knowing smirk.

"A loser," I elaborate. "You got anything stronger?"

"I'll get the whiskey."

We all watch as he leaves the room then I finally turn back to Lori and her stalker. His knuckles are white from gripping her hand so hard, the needy bastard. I give it another month until she needs to file a restraining order against him. "Well, this is cozy," I say.

He smiles but she doesn't. "Aren't you going to introduce us properly, babe?" he asks.

Where's the whiskey? Maybe I could take a drink every time he calls her babe. "Yeah, *babe*," I say. "Introduce us." New guy laughs, completely oblivious to everything. I'd feel sorry for him if he wasn't fucking my girl.

Lori scowls, looking like she would rather be anywhere but here. "John, this is Buzz. Buzz, John."

Of course he's a *John*. A boring name for a boring man.

"Interesting name," he says.

"Shame I can't say the same about yours."

"Touché," he says, laughing. "So is Buzz your real name or nickname?"

"It might as well be my real name."

"What's the story behind it?"

"Maybe another time," Lori says with a warning glance in my direction. "I wonder what's taking so long with the food…"

"When I come, I shout 'to infinity and beyond'."

He looks confused. "Excuse me?"

You heard.

Mason walks back into the room juggling the whiskey and a huge serving plate of lamb. "My nickname. When I come, I shout 'to infinity and beyond'. You know, like what Buzz says in *Toy Story*." Lori closes her eyes and I can't help but wonder if she's taking a trip down memory lane.

He looks confused. "I've never seen *Toy Story*."

"Well you're missing out."

"If you can't guess, he was drunk at the time," Mason says as he places the lamb down. "He'd been watching Toy Story earlier that day. He only said it that one time but that's all it takes for a nickname to stick,

70

right? It's been about ten years but it's not something that your friends are going to let you forget in a hurry."

"I've said it more than once, actually," I correct him while looking at Lori. Her eyes shoot open as her cheeks turn red.

"Dude, TMI," Mason replies as he pours the whiskey.

John laughs. "Well it's certainly a good story for a dinner party. I'm not sure it's one to tell the grandchildren though."

Fuck you, John. I can tell my future grandchildren whatever the hell I want. Maybe one day I'll tell them about the time their crazy-ass grandmother decided to date a loser called John before she came to her senses and got back with me. "I'm sure they would be too busy thanking me. If it wasn't for me, their mom or dad wouldn't be alive."

"Touché."

New game - drink every time he says 'babe' or 'touché'.

Mason hands me my drink right on time. I take a long drink and then lick my lips when I see Lori watching me. Her eyes fall to my mouth and I want to ask her if she's remembering all the times it's been on her. All the things my tongue has done to her.

"Anyone else for whiskey?" Mason asks.

They both shake their heads in response. "No thanks, buddy," John says. "I'll wait for the wine."

Buddy? So now he's trying to steal my best friend too? I don't think so, *buddy*.

"So, what do you do for work, Buzz?"

"I work for Mason," I tell him. "I'm his bitch."

"It's true," Mason adds.

"What about you? What do you do?"

"I'm a doctor."

Of course he is. "What do you specialize in?" I ask.

"Dentistry."

So that explains the ridiculously white teeth. "Oh, you're a dentist. I thought you were a real doctor."

"Don't be rude," Lori says. "John works extremely hard."

"I'm not doubting that. I'm just being honest. I thought he was a real doctor. You don't exactly save lives by whitening people's teeth."

"I carry out more complicated procedures than that."

"It's hardly open-heart surgery though is it, doc?"

"And what would you know about broken hearts, Buzz?" Lori asks with hurt in her eyes.

"More than you'd think," I reply.

More silence. More unspoken words.

"John is introducing me to his mother this weekend," she says, and it feels like a test.

"That's nice," I lie, trying my best to act cool but ruin it by blurting out, "A little quick though, don't you think?"

"Not really. It's just the next step. It's what happens in normal relationships."

"I wouldn't know. I've never liked normal. What comes after that? Boring sex and white picket fences?"

Her eyes go wide but John laughs. "You don't need to worry about our sex life, if you know what I'm saying."

"Oh, I'm not worried." *I'm sure she has lots of fun faking her orgasms for you.* "Hey, that reminds me…it's Thursday today. You up for drinks after this, Lor?"

She looks like she wants to kill me and fuck me at the same time. "What happens on Thursday's?" John asks.

Lori begins to mumble, presumably trying to make something up but I cut her off. "Throwback Thursday. It means we're allowed to sleep with our ex's, no strings attached. What do you say?"

"Absolutely not," she says through gritted teeth.

"Come on, not even for old time's sake?"

"That's enough," Mason warns.

I laugh. "Come on, guys, lighten up. I'm just joking around."

Sophia walks in right on cue, holding a bottle of wine and two plates. "Mase, can you take the plates from me before I drop them?"

He's already done it by the time she's even finished her sentence. It's like they can read each other's minds. "Of course. I was going to come back and help but I thought I might get told off again for abandoning our guests."

In other words, he's been instructed to babysit me.

They place potatoes and vegetables on the table and then Sophia grins nervously. "Okay, so here we have a carved roast leg of lamb with basil and mint pesto paired with a 2010 Pinot Noir."

"Excellent choice," John says. I lean over and begin to scoop potatoes onto my plate. "May we start?" he asks, which makes me look like I have no manners whatsoever.

"I'm pretty sure she didn't spend the last few hours cooking this feast just for us to stare at it," I say as I pile my plate with lamb.

John chuckles. "Hungry?"

I look at Lori. "Ravenous." I take a bite of lamb and then moan. "It tastes *so* good." I'm mostly doing it for Lori's sake, but it does actually taste nice too.

Sophia beams. "Yay! Thank god for that."

Lori continues to watch me eat, her eyes darker than they were moments before. After a few seconds, John says something, but I can't make out the words and apparently neither can she. "Babe?" he says.

I take a drink.

"Huh?" she asks, dragging her eyes away from mine.

"I asked if that's enough food for you."

She eyes the tiny portion. "No. I'm actually hungry." I laugh as she scoops more food onto her plate. It's obvious that he doesn't know how to satisfy her appetite.

"This is delicious," Mason says. "Looks like I have a chef on my hands. Now you can cook me dinner every night."

"Watch it, we haven't exchanged any vows yet."

Everybody laughs. "I don't want to make your head any bigger," Lori says. "But the lamb is cooked to perfection."

"You're right," I say. "It's perfect. It reminds me of your tattoo."

She frowns. "My tattoo? What are you talking about?"

"Your favorite book quote." She knows exactly what I mean but I carry on for John's sake. "*And so the lion fell in love with the lamb.*"

Everybody is silent until John starts to choke on his food. *Can't he at least die quietly?*

Lori blushes and shakes her head in warning as she pats him on the back. He coughs for about half a minute before taking a long drink of water. "I'm okay," he says. "I just think I misheard Buzz, that's all."

"Nah, you didn't."

He narrows his eyes at me. "Remind me how you two know each other."

Sophia sighs. "Oh, you haven't worked it out yet?" I ask. "We used to date."

"We used to be friends," Lori answers at the same time as me.

"Friends with benefits," I say as I pop a potato into my mouth. "You can't forget that part, sweetheart."

"You dated?" John turns to her, looking genuinely surprised. "How long for?"

"A few months."

"Five," I clarify.

"Three."

"Five in total."

"But officially three," she says.

I shrug. "Five total."

"On and off."

I take a drink. "But mostly on."

"How long ago was this?" he asks. "How many years ago?"

I laugh. "Years? It was six *months a*go. How long have you been dating?"

"Four months," he answers.

"And she hasn't mentioned me?" I clutch my chest. "I'm offended."

"I don't like to dwell on the past," she says.

"Yes, I can see that. You move quickly. I guess it shouldn't come as a surprise. You always did like it fast." I'm pretty sure this will go down as the most awkward dinner party in history.

John clears his throat and begins to stroke her hand. "Well I guess it's nice that we can all have dinner together. No hard feelings, right?"

"Absolutely not," Sophia says as she raises her glass in the air. "To good friends and no hard feelings."

We all cheers and take a quick drink before I hold my glass back up in the air. "And to Throwback Thursday, where *hard* feelings are not only welcomed but necessary."

Mason and Sophia half laugh, half cringe as if they have no idea how to react to my toast. John follows their lead and chuckles as he holds his glass up to mine. "To Throwback Thursday but staying well clear of certain ex's who are no good for us."

Lori almost chokes on her drink. I knock my glass against his a little too hard, causing his wine to spill out onto both him and the table. "Oh, I can't make any promises." He laughs along with me but looks nervous as he dabs at his jacket.

Good. He should be.

Lori stands up. "Excuse us. Buzz, can I have a quick word with you?"

"Of course." I wink at John as I follow her out of the room.

"What the hell are you doing?" she asks as soon as we're in the kitchen.

"I almost forgot how sexy you are when you're angry."

"Jesus, can you be serious for one goddamn minute?"

I groan as I rearrange the contents of my boxer shorts. "Yes, but can you stop being mad at me? You know the effect it has on me."

Her eyes go wide. "Oh my god. Are you actually getting turned on by this?"

"No. I'm getting turned on by *you*."

She glances down at my dick and then huffs as she turns around and walks over to the sink. She hunches over and my gaze falls to her ass, which does nothing to calm the party inside my pants.

"Why are you here?" she asks.

"Because I wanted to see you. What are you doing here with him? Why are you dating him?"

"I don't have to answer any of your questions."

"He's not your type."

She turns around to look at me. "And what *is* my type?"

"Me." She rolls her eyes. "What? You know it's true. Tall, toned and tats. My tattoos used to drive you crazy, remember?"

"Used to, Buzz. *Used to.*" I unzip my trousers. "What the hell are you doing?" She can act like she doesn't want me anymore, but her eyes are full of desire. I pull down my jeans and boxer shorts until the tattoos just below my hip bones are showing. Her eyes continue south. "You always used to say these were your favorite tattoos of mine."

She closes her eyes and when she reopens them, they're sad. "Again – used to. I used to say a lot of things, Buzz. We both *used to.*"

"Why are you with him, Lori? I'm being serious. I want to know why. Name three things you like about him."

"He's nice. And trustworthy."

"That's two things."

"He's a nice guy, Buzz."

"That's still only two. See, you can't even list three things."

She sighs. "Do you really want to do this? Is this how you want to play it?" I raise an eyebrow. "Fine. Three things. He's nice, he's trustworthy and he's *great* in bed."

I hold on to the countertop to steady myself. "Bullshit."

"What?"

"A guy like him doesn't know his way around a woman's body."

"A guy like him?"

"A sap. He's a *dentist,* for fucks sake."

She crosses her arms. "You're right, he *is* a dentist and he has exceptional *oral* skills."

Ouch. The thought of another man touching her, *tasting* her, makes me crazy. I don't hide it very well as she sighs. "Let's not do this. Let's not hurt each other any more than we already have, okay?"

"It's a little too late for that."

"It's a little too late for any of this, Buzz. Six months too late."

"It's never too late for us."

She frowns. "For us? Have you heard yourself? There *is* no us. I haven't heard from you in six months.

Why now? Why all of a sudden do you think you can come here and start quizzing me about my new relationship? What's changed?"

"Another man is in your bed, that's what has changed."

"So you don't want me, you just don't want anybody else to have me. Is that what it is?"

"You know that's not what it is. I've always wanted you and I've never wanted you around other men. That's the only reason we broke up - because you wouldn't leave your job. Because trapping other men was more important than keeping me."

"That's not true."

"Well that's what happened."

"You gave me an ultimatum, *that's* what happened. You didn't trust me, *that's* what happened. And your jealously and ego were more important than keeping me, *that's what happened.*"

I slam my fist down on the counter. "Damn it, Lori. That's not true."

She takes a step closer to me. "I didn't choose my job over you."

We stare at each other, our chests rising and falling in unison. "Tell me something. Is *he* okay with what you do?" She looks down at her feet. "You've got to be kidding me. He doesn't know?"

"I...I don't..."

"Is everything okay?" Sophia asks. "I heard a bang."

"Everything's fine," Lori replies, keeping her eyes on mine.

"I'm glad *you* seem to think so."

Sophia sighs. "John's in the next room. I don't think this is the time or the place."

"Oh, come on," I say. "We all know he's just the rebound guy."

"I'm sure you know all about rebounds. I dread to think of how many women you've slept with in the last six months. Have you successfully worked your way through everybody in San Francisco? Is that why you've come back? Are you doubling up now?"

I narrow my eyes. "I haven't had sex with anybody since you, Lor."

She laughs. "That's the funniest thing I've heard all year. Do you honestly expect me to believe that?"

"Yes, I do, because it's the truth. I would never lie to you."

"That's where you're wrong because you *did* lie to me."

"When?"

"You told me you'd never leave me." Her eyes begin to fill with tears.

"Come on now, don't get upset," Sophia says as she takes hold of Lori's hand. "This is the first time you've seen each other since you broke up. Emotions are high. We all need to slow down." I take a step backwards and Sophia's eyes shoot down to my jeans which are still unzipped. "We need to slow it *right down*. Do you think it's a good idea to go back out there?"

"No, it isn't," Lori answers for me. "Just go home, Buzz. Or better yet, go and find one of your ex's to spend your beloved Throwback Thursday with. Lord knows there are enough of them."

"There's one standing right in front of me."

"And there are hundreds of others out there."

"I don't want anybody else."

She throws her hands in the air and turns to Sophia. "Have you heard him? You don't want me, Buzz. You're just horny. You're confusing your sexual frustration with actual feelings. Go and fuck somebody to get it out of your system then we can all move on with our lives."

I narrow my eyes. "Is that what you really want?"

She hesitates before storming out of the room.

"She didn't answer the question," I say to Sophia.

"Buzz…"

"We both know that she's not happy with him."

She sighs. "But she *wants* to be and that's got to count for something. If she didn't like him, she wouldn't be wasting either of their time. And as much as you want to believe it, she isn't a rebound kind of girl. I've always rooted for you guys but it just didn't work out. Maybe it's time to take a step back and let John have his shot."

"I can't just sit back and watch."

"Then don't. Don't watch."

"I can't keep my eyes closed forever."

"Not forever. Just until you're ready."

I raise an eyebrow. "Like I said, I can't keep my eyes closed forever."

"Oh, Buzz," she says, her eyes filling with concern. "I didn't even realize you felt this way. I mean, I know you both had a hard time after the break-up but I didn't know you felt this strongly. None of us did. No wonder Lori's so confused and caught off guard tonight. Why didn't you say something sooner? You could have tried to work things out."

"That's why I'm here now."

"But it's been six months."

"Believe me, I know. I've felt worse with each month. I drank the first few weeks away and then my therapist told me to put some distance between us."

"Your therapist?"

"I've been seeing one every week."

"You should have said something. Does Mason know any of this?"

"No."

"Buzz, it's not good to keep everything to yourself."

"Why do you think I hired a therapist?"

"I wouldn't have let you come tonight if I knew you still had so many feelings. Jesus, it must be horrible for you to see them together."

"It is." I sigh. "Tell me his last name and I'll leave."

"Why do you want to know?" she asks, one eyebrow raised.

"I want to run a background check on him so I can at least sleep at night."

"Buzz, no. You don't need to know any more than you already do."

"Soph, please. Let me just check the guy out. It's for her own safety."

"Then you'll back off?"

"If that's what she wants."

She crosses her arms. "It's Crown."

"You're kidding me?"

"No?"

"John *Crown*. Is that why he became a dentist? What a loser."

"Buzz," she warns.

I hold my hands up. "Just saying."

"Please don't do anything stupid."

"Would I?" I lean in and kiss her on the cheek. "Thanks for tonight. The lamb was delicious." I wink. "And I didn't even have to fake it. Tell Mason I'll see him tomorrow." I begin to walk away. "And tell Lori how great I am." She tries to hide her grin as I slip out of the room.

I close my apartment door and then bang my head against it several times.

Tonight was a lot harder than I was expecting. Seeing Lori with another man killed me. It extinguished a fire inside of me but also ignited another - one which will destroy everything in its path until she's back in my arms. I feel deflated yet determined. She still loves me, I can feel it. Hell, I could *see* it. John must be blind if he couldn't see it too.

I drag my hands down my face as I try not to think about her going home with him. Maybe I should just get it over with and tell him about her job. Tell him that she gets paid to expose cheating men. I'm pretty sure he wouldn't be okay with that. I'm pretty sure *most* men wouldn't be. I have no idea why she's started a new relationship when she can't even be honest with them.

I take a deep breath and walk over to the sofa, which will be my bed for the night. As fucked up as it sounds, I can't even face looking at a bed tonight. Not when I know that Lori will be warming another man's. It's almost enough to make me throw up.

I fall back onto the sofa and pull my cell out of my pocket. I do a quick Google search of his name and it takes 0.05 seconds to find out where he works.

Looks like I'll be taking a little trip to the dentist tomorrow.

CHAPTER TWELVE

Mason sighs. "For the hundredth time - no, she didn't talk about you after you left. Not to me, anyway."

"So does that mean she spoke to Sophia about me?"

"I don't know."

"Don't lie to me."

"I'm not lying. The world doesn't revolve around you, you know."

"It doesn't?"

"Not at all." He looks at his watch. "Come on, let's go and get some lunch."

"I'm skipping lunch today."

He raises an eyebrow. "You never skip lunch. What's wrong with you? Are you sick?"

"No. I have an appointment."

"An appointment for what?"

I shrug. "It's personal. Nothing important."

"Ahhh, I think I know what it is."

"You do?"

"Yeah." He lowers his voice. "STD check. Or is it for treatment?"

I throw my pen at him. "Fuck you! I don't have an STD."

"Well the last time you had a *personal appointment*…"

"It was one time, man. One time. Plus, it was about three years ago."

He holds his hands up in innocence. "Do you want me to get you any lunch while you go to your top secret, *personal* appointment?" He uses air quotes. "The one which *isn't* anything to do with STD's?"

"You're a dick."

"Yes, they'll probably want to see your dick. That's how it works."

"And how would you know, asshole?"

He scratches his chin. "Hmmm, yeah, they might want to see your asshole too."

I stand up to leave. "I quit."

"Hallelujah! I've been waiting for this moment forever." He pushes the intercom button on his phone. "Natalia, can you arrange to have Buzz's office packed up, please? And could you also type up a job description for his replacement? He doesn't do much so it won't take you very long."

"You're a shitty friend."

He laughs. "I'll pick you up your usual chicken salad."

"Nah, don't bother. There's a sandwich shop next door to the dentist."

"The dentist? That's where you're going?" His eyes widen when realization kicks in. "Buzz…no…"

I open the door. "Laters."

"Don't do it."

"Do what? I'm due a check-up."

"It's not going to change anything."

"Maybe not." I shrug. "But at least my teeth will be whiter."

A little bell chimes to signal my arrival. A pretty blonde receptionist looks up at me and smiles. Oh, this should be a piece of cake.

"Hi there, can I help you?"

I look at her name tag and try my best not to stare at her tits. "I sure hope so, Hannah."

"Do you have an appointment?"

"Actually, I was just passing by and thought I'd try my luck. Do you have any cancellations for today? I have a spare couple of hours."

"I'm pretty sure Dr Crown is fully booked for today."

"Aww, come on," I say, looking her up and down. "I'm sure you can *fit me in*."

She giggles. "I'll see what I can do. Would you like to take a seat?"

I sit on the edge of her desk and give her my best cheeky grin. "I'd love to."

"He has an emergency appointment available in about an hour, right before his lunch break." She lowers her voice. "I'm not supposed to use them unless absolutely necessary."

"I won't tell if you don't."

She smiles. "What's your name? I'll find you on the system and get you booked in."

Don't bother; you're not going to find me. "Buzz."

"That's an unusual name."

"Have you ever seen the movie *Toy Story*?" She's probably way too young.

The door behind her opens and John walks out. He frowns when he sees me. "Buzz? I didn't expect to see you again so soon."

"Right back at you. I didn't realize you worked here."

"My name is on the sign outside..."

"Oh, I didn't look. I was in the area and noticed that it was a dentists office."

"Has my next appointment arrived yet, Hannah?" She shakes her head. "Then come on in, Buzz. I don't have long though."

"Great." I wink at Hannah. "Thanks."

"So what can I do for you?" he asks once the door closes behind us.

You can start by breaking up with Lori.

I walk over to his desk and pick up a framed photograph of her. "How long did you say you've been together?" I ask, gesturing to it.

He folds his arms. "Four months."

And he's already got a framed photograph of her? *What a loser.* I frown as I look closer. Wait a minute…

"When did you take this photo?" I ask, even though I know the answer.

"Oh, I didn't take it. I just stole it off her Facebook." *Well that's just downright creepy.* "It's my favorite picture of her. She looks so happy."

Okay, I need to set him straight. "She *was* happy. I know that because I'm the one who took the photo." It's the first time I've seen him look pissed off. *Welcome to the club.* "I can see why it's your favorite. Did you know that she's naked in it from the waist down? Oh, of course you didn't know. How would you? Nobody would know except for me and her. That's why she looks so happy. Jesus, I used to get a hard-on every time I logged into Facebook and saw it."

"What are you doing here, Buzz?" he asks through gritted teeth.

We stare at each other for a long moment and I decide to just lay it all on the line. "I want you to step down."

His eyebrows nearly reach his hairline which is a huge achievement considering how much he's receding. "Step down?"

"You've only known her for four months. We have history. Unfinished business."

"I understand how hard this must be for you, but you need to accept that she's in love with me now."

"And *you* need to accept that she's in love with me too."

"Has she told you that?"

"No."

"Then maybe we should wait until the words come out of her mouth."

"And they will. Couldn't you feel the tension last night?"

"You're her ex. She hasn't seen you in six months. Of course there's going to be a weird atmosphere."

"Was she acting differently after you left Mason and Sophia's last night?"

He shrugs. "I don't see where you're going with this…"

"I'm just trying to find out whether she was thinking about me while going home with you."

"Wow. It's all coming out now, huh?"

"Man to man. Do you really want to be the rebound guy? Plan B? Do you want to be somebody's safe bet?"

"I want to be somebody's someone, which is more than you have right now." He walks over to the door. "I think it's time for you to leave."

I take a seat in his obnoxious, oversized leather chair which is probably to make up for the fact that he has a tiny dick. It must make him feel like a real man. "Nah, I think I'll stay. You obviously don't understand the seriousness of the situation."

"Are you threatening me?"

"No. You'd know if I was threatening you. I'm hoping it doesn't get that far."

"Do I need to call the cops and have them remove you from my office?"

"If you're a little bitch who can't deal with their own problems then yeah, you probably should."

"I don't know what you want me to do or say, Buzz. Do you want to fight me? Is that why you came here? Do you want to make yourself feel better by breaking my face?"

"That *would* make me feel better but no, I didn't come here for a fight. I came to give you the opportunity to bow out gracefully, before this gets messy. If I were you, I would get out now. It's called self-preservation."

"I trust Lori. I don't believe that she would ever hurt me. I think that you're the one who needs to step down. You need to move on."

"That's never going to happen. There's really no need to make this any harder than it has to be."

"Does Lori know that you're here?"

"No, she has nothing to do with this."

"I wonder what she's going to say when she finds out that her boyfriend was threatened by her ex?"

She's probably going to think that you're a little rat. "I'm just trying to make this easier for everyone involved."

"No. You're trying to steal my girlfriend."

Well at least we're on the same page now. "Is she honest with you?" He nods. "So she's told you about her job?"

"Of course. She works in the library across town."

I laugh. "No she doesn't. You don't even know the half of it."

"What do you mean? I've seen her working there. I've met her on my lunch break and walked her home a couple of times."

How sweet. "It's all just a cover up. She's really a honey trapper. She gets paid to trap cheating men."

His frown transforms into a smug smile. "She doesn't do that anymore."

I freeze. So he *does* know about it. "What?"

"She quit about two months ago. She started working at the library right away."

My head starts to spin and it feels like the walls are closing in on me. She quit for him? *For him?*

"We don't keep secrets, Buzz."

I shake free from my trance. "Except when they're about me, apparently."

"The past should stay in the past. I don't doubt that you still have feelings for her but she's with me now. Unless she tells me to back off, then I'll be here to stay."

I can't listen to any more of this bullshit. I have more important things to deal with. I stand up and walk over to the door, throwing the framed photo of her in the trash on my way out. Childish, I know, but it was either that or throw it at his head. I don't think Mason would be too pleased if I missed this afternoon's meeting because I was in jail. Besides, I took the fucking photo so I get to decide what happens with it. He steps to the side, allowing me to reach for the door handle. I turn to look at him as I push down on it. "Don't say I didn't warn you."

CHAPTER THIRTEEN

I'm about to call Mason but hesitate and carry on scrolling until I reach Sophia's name. Nobody knows Lori better than she does. If anyone can give me answers, it'll be her.

"Hello?" she answers almost immediately.

"She quit for him?" I ask in greeting, unable to bite my tongue.

"Oh, shit."

"My thoughts exactly."

"Who told you?" she asks.

"Who do you think told me?"

"Lori?"

"Try again."

She groans. "You've been to see John?"

"Yep."

"Oh my god, no."

"Oh my god, yes," I reply.

"Why?"

"Why do people usually visit a dentist, Soph? I went to tell him to back the fuck away from Lori, *obviously*."

"Buzz! You promised you'd leave them alone."

"No I didn't. I promised to back off if that's what she wants. *Is* that what she wants?" I spot the library building in the distance. "Because now would be a good fucking time to tell me."

I carry on walking in silence for a few seconds until she answers. "To be completely honest, I don't know what she wants. I don't even think *she* knows what she wants."

"Then until she figures her shit out, I'm not going anywhere. Why didn't you tell me that she's quit honey trapping?"

She sighs. "I didn't see the point. I didn't want to re-open any wounds. I thought you had moved on.

Besides, Lori should have been the one to tell you – not me and definitely not John."

"I can't believe she quit for him. I can't understand it."

"She didn't quit *for him*. Since when would Lori do something just to please a man?"

"Do you really want me to answer that? Because I've got a long list of things she's done purely to satisfy me."

"Oh, good," she replies. "You can't be *too* upset if you're still making jokes."

"I'll let you know how it goes later."

"What are you talking about?"

"I'm about to go and speak to her now."

"Maybe you should give it a little time? You know, think about what you want to say first."

"I know exactly what I want to say. It's too late for that anyway, I'm already here." I push open the huge wooden doors.

"Already where?"

"At the library."

"Buzz, no. Not at her work."

"Oh, come on. What's the worst that can happen? It *is* a library after all. It's not as if she's going to shout at me or throw a book at my head…she respects them too much for that. God forbid a cover ever got damaged or a page was folded. I'll catch you later."

"Wait…"

I end the call and head straight over to the help desk. "Hello. I'm looking for Lori."

The old lady peers over the top of her glasses. "Who?"

"Lori Campbell. She started working here about two months ago. She's about five foot five, brunette and beautiful."

She frowns and shouts over to one of her colleagues. "Do you know somebody called Lori?

Apparently she started working here a few weeks ago." She smirks. "Brunette and beautiful."

The younger woman shakes her head. "Nope, not that I know of."

"Maybe it's her day off?" I ask, unable to hide my disappointment.

"I think you've got the wrong library. I work here most days and I haven't met any new starters. Maybe you should try Maxwell library."

"Maxwell? I didn't know there was more than one library in town."

She laughs. "It's the library over at the University of San Francisco."

"Thanks, I'll try there."

Two libraries in one day? If that doesn't impress Lori, I don't know what will.

Twenty minutes later, I walk through a set of sliding doors and instantly know that this is where I'm meant to be. *Of course* this is where Lori works. I get a lump in my throat at how perfect it is for her. It's bigger than the last library and way more modern. It's full of metal staircases and people sitting inside little white pods reading their books. I carry on walking and chuckle to myself when I notice a conveyor belt which snakes around the whole bottom floor, displaying books for readers to grab and take home. No wonder everything is painted bright white – it is absolute heaven for book lovers.

Just as I'm admiring a piece of artwork used in a book called *Confess,* I see Lori walking towards me. She couldn't look any more like a librarian if she tried. She's wearing a white button-up blouse and a chequered knee-length skirt which turns me on way more than it should. Her hair is scraped into a bun on the top of her head and her glasses perch on the end of her nose.

She gasps when she notices me and drops the huge stack of books that she was carrying. I laugh as I bend down to help her pick them up. "This would have been the perfect way to meet for the first time. Isn't this the kind of thing you book lovers dream about?" I lean in closer. "This is the second library I've been to today. Does that turn you on as much as your outfit is turning me on?"

She swallows hard as she takes the last of the books from me. "What are you doing here, Buzz?"

"Well I'm not here for the books, that's for sure." She closes her eyes when I reach out and tuck a loose strand of hair behind her ear. "You look beautiful."

When she opens them again, I see a mix of emotions. "Why are you here?"

"To talk."

"We said everything we needed to say last night."

"Oh, I'm pretty sure *you* didn't."

"What do you mean by that?" she asks.

"Why didn't you tell me that you've quit trapping?"

Her eyes widen. "Who told you?"

"It doesn't matter. What matters is that *you* weren't the one to tell me."

"What did you want me to do, Buzz? Text you and tell you even though we hadn't spoken in months?"

"Yes, that's exactly what I wanted you to do."

"And what would I have said?"

"How about, 'Hey, Buzz. It's Lori here. I've quit trapping so we can get back together now.' Something like that would have been fine."

She shakes her head. "It doesn't change anything."

"Are you joking? It changes *everything*."

"I was already with John."

"I don't understand why you quit for him but you wouldn't for me."

"I didn't quit for him. I quit for *me*. That's the whole point, Buzz. I quit when *I* was ready."

"Which was only a month or two after we broke up. If you knew you were going to quit eventually, why didn't you just do it when you knew I was struggling with it?"

"Because you weren't just *struggling* with it, you couldn't handle it. Besides, I didn't have any plans of quitting then."

"So what made you change your mind?"

She shrugs. "I couldn't carry on doing the job forever and I saw how happy Sophia was after she quit. It was like a huge weight was taken off her shoulders. She was free to live her life. An *honest* life. I saw how happy she was with Mason and when they got engaged, it made me realize that I want that too."

"With John?"

"John had nothing to do with my decision." She sighs. "You need to leave. I'm working."

"Come over to my place tonight."

"We both know that's not a good idea."

"Why not? Because you can't trust yourself around me?"

I follow her as she walks over to a table and places the books on top. She flexes her fingers. "Stop making this harder than it has to be."

"You're the one making things hard. Stop messing around with John."

"I'm not *messing around* with anybody. I really like him."

"Oh, come on. You're settling. Even if you don't want to be with me, please don't settle for him. You deserve so much more."

"You're so rude, do you know that? John is an amazing person. He's so patient and kind. I'm definitely not *settling* by being with him."

"Are you in love with him?" She doesn't answer. She doesn't do anything. I'm pretty sure she's holding her breath, just like I am. "Are you in love with him?" I ask again, crouching down until we're at eye level.

"I'm not having this conversation with you."

"Why not?"

"Because!"

"Because what?"

She takes a step closer to me and pokes a finger into my chest. "Because what you're doing is not okay, Buzz." More prodding as she adds, "This. Is. Not. Okay."

"I'll tell you what's not okay; seeing you with another man when we both know that you belong to me."

"There you go again with your alpha bullshit. I don't *belong* to anybody."

"It's not bullshit. It's the truth. We belong together."

"We're dangerous together."

"Says who?"

"Me! We're gasoline and fire, Buzz."

I can feel the frustration building up inside of me. "Gasoline and fire? Well if I'm gasoline then John is a big cold bucket of water. I saw you with him last night, remember? Your eyes were dead when you looked at him. There *was* no fire. There wasn't even a flicker. I'd always choose to take a risk over playing it safe. All those nights we used to spend talking about our future…not once did a forty-year-old dentist come into that."

"There you go again being rude! Leave John out of this!"

"*You* leave John out of this!"

"Maybe I don't want to. Maybe I *want* some safety."

"Do you love him?" I ask again.

She begins to walk away but I grab hold of her arm and spin her back around to face me. "Answer my question, Lori. Do you love him?"

"I don't know. I thought I did and then..." she trails off.

"And then?"

"And then you bulldozed your way back into my life last night. Now my head is all messed up."

"So then I haven't lost you yet?"

"I didn't say that."

"You're not saying a whole lot."

"Because this isn't fair on John."

"Fuck John!" I reply a little too loud, catching the attention of some people nearby. I lower my voice and lean in closer. "John gets to hold you and kiss you. He gets to make love to you. Trust me when I say that John is doing just fine."

She sighs. "I need time, Buzz. Please give me some time."

"You've had six months."

"No. Give me some time to see how things go with John. I *want* to find out where it could go."

"You've just told me that you're not sure how you feel. Forgive me but there's no way in hell that I'm going to step back and watch you fall in love with another man. I'll never stop fighting for you, Lori. I stopped fighting six months ago and you found your way into another man's bed. Into another man's heart. Never again."

"You need to let me figure this out on my own. If we're truly meant to be together then we will find our way back to each other."

My heart is beating out of my chest but deep down, I know that she's right. I need to be smart about this. Even though it kills me, I need to respect what she wants and help her reach the right decision rather than pressure her into it. I want her to *want* to be with me. I want her to see how boring life is with John so that when she comes back to me, she knows she's made the right decision. I take her hand in mine and hold it up against my chest. "I hope you find your way back to me." She rolls her eyes when I add, "Really fucking soon."

Six hours later, she came back.

CHAPTER FOURTEEN

I groan when there's a knock at my front door. I've just spent the last twenty minutes browsing the internet for the perfect librarian porn and was about to start when I was rudely interrupted. I consider ignoring them but whoever it is knocks again, as well as ringing the doorbell.

I stand up and adjust my boxers in an attempt to hide my raging hard-on but fail miserably. I reach for my pants and begrudgingly put them back on as I glance at the two sexy librarians on my laptop screen.

"Okay, okay, I'm coming!" I yell as the knocking gets louder. "Well, I will be as soon as you leave me in peace," I mutter under my breath. Haven't they heard of cell phones? By the time I reach the door, the knocking has turned into full-on banging. "Calm the fuck down!" I shout as I turn the lock and push down on the handle.

"I will *not* calm down!" Lori replies as she pushes past me, storming straight into the kitchen. My dick twitches at the sight of her still wearing her work clothes. *Down, boy.* The fake librarian pornstars have nothing on her. I close the door and find her pacing up and down. "This ends now!" she says.

"What does?"

She gestures between us. "*This.* All of it. Everything was fine until yesterday."

"Care to elaborate?"

"Stop threatening John. He's done nothing wrong."

I roll my eyes. "I didn't threaten anybody."

"Yes, you did. He told me."

"Oh, he *told* you so that must mean it's true."

"How dare you go into his work and threaten him!"

"I didn't threaten him. And I have every right to go to his public place of work."

"No, you don't! Stay away from him. It's bad enough that you came to *my* work but don't involve him too. Did it make you feel big and tough by threatening him?"

"For fuck sake, Lori! How many times do I have to tell you? I *didn't* threaten him and if he told you that I did then he's a lying piece of shit."

"Why the hell would he lie about it?"

"Because he's trying to make me look bad and because he's scared of losing you." *And he can probably sense that it's about to happen.*

"And what about the vandalism?"

"Wait, what?"

"You vandalized his office." I can't help but laugh at how ridiculous that sounds. He's really gone to town on playing the victim card. "I'm glad you think that this is funny."

"It's laughable. I didn't vandalize his office."

"For a start, you threw his photo frame in the bin."

"A photo of you! One that I took! So technically that was mine to do whatever the hell I wanted with it."

"What are you talking about?"

103

"Oh, he didn't tell you which photo was inside the frame?" She looks confused. "He printed it off your Facebook. The picture where you're sitting on my bed. You know - the one when you're half naked. He has no right to have that on his desk."

She blushes. "What about his door?"

"His door?"

"He said you damaged his office door. What did you do? Kick it? Punch it?"

Oh. I try my best to keep a straight face. "No...I altered his name plaque."

"What do you mean you altered it?"

"I'll admit, it was childish of me. But he threatened to call the cops after the photo thing, so I was pissed off."

"What did you do?"

"I changed his name from Crown to Clown." She rolls her eyes. "What? I think it suits him better."

"Buzz..."

I hold my hands up. "I'm sorry. I shouldn't have done it."

"No, you shouldn't have. Just leave him out of this from now on."

"You've only been together for a few months and he's secretly framing photographs of you. You've got to admit, that's pretty fucking creepy."

"Well you and I have been broken up for six months but you're stalking my new boyfriend. You've got to admit, *that's* pretty creepy too."

"I hate hearing you call him that." Now I'm the one who starts to pace up and down. "Please don't refer to him as that when you're around me."

"What? My boyfriend?"

I flinch. "Yes. I hate it."

"But that's what he is."

"I'm well aware of that. Did you purposely look for a guy who was the complete opposite of me in every single way?"

She folds her arms across her chest and lifts her chin up. "Maybe. Maybe I needed something different. You broke up with me because of my job. You didn't love me enough to see past it. Excuse me for not wanting to go through that again."

"That's bullshit."

"And then to top it all off, you cut me out of your life for six months. Not once did you call to check how I was doing. Not once."

"I've been trying to sort my shit out." *And trying to better myself for you.* The truth is that I've always been so sure that we would end up back together that I never felt the need to worry about other men. I wrongly assumed that we would both stay single until we reunited. And in my head, it was always a matter of *when*, not *if*.

"And how has that worked out for you?"

I shrug. "Only time will tell."

"Well I refuse to be your guinea pig. I'm getting too old to play games. I want a life with somebody. Not just great sex or a couple of good years together. I want commitment. I want honesty and loyalty."

"I've always been honest and loyal."

"You joked about white picket fences last night but that's what I want. I want a cute little house with a swing out on the front porch. I want marriage and babies. I want it all, Buzz."

There goes my hard-on. I run a hand across my jaw. "I might want that too, some day."

"You might...but you might not. I'm edging closer to thirty. I don't want to waste any more time."

"So you're settling down with the first guy who wants kids? Come on, Lori. I know you. You've always followed your heart, not your brain. You want the fireworks and the fairytale. You don't want a sperm donor. This is your life you're talking about, not a business venture."

"You're right. I do want the fairytale. I live for the happy ever after. Books are my life. But do you know what I realized the other day? That I'm always attracted to the alpha's. I always fall hard for the bad boys. I never give gentlemen enough credit. But I've finally accepted that fiction isn't the same as real life. We don't always get the whirlwind romance and that's okay. I don't need the drama and plot twists to have a fulfilling relationship. If I want my happy ever after, I have to go out and get it. I have to work for it. Maybe it'll be a slow burn instead of insta-love. Maybe it'll be gentle kisses instead of the hottest sex of my life. Maybe it won't be the happy ever after that I always imagined but it'll still be *mine*."

I raise an eyebrow. "The hottest sex of your life, huh?"

"See. You can't be serious."

"I did it on purpose. I was just trying to make you laugh." *And trying to erase the image of somebody else giving you gentle kisses.* "I'm sorry. I'm listening to what you're saying. I'm taking it all in."

"I can see a future with John. I can picture what my life would look like."

"And you can't picture your life with me?"

Her eyes turn sad. "No, I can't. I don't even know what tomorrow would look like with you and that scares the absolute crap out of me."

"Then let me show you. Let's make our future together."

She shakes her head. "You told me that you don't believe in marriage."

"I don't. I don't see why a piece of paper makes any difference. I saw all the shit it caused my mom and dad and then I watched Mason's marriage fall apart. I saw how it chipped away at him until he was a shell of a man. I don't see why so much importance is placed on marriage these days when divorces are handed out so willingly. What's the fucking point?"

"It shows commitment to a person."

"I can show commitment in other ways. I could give you a life more beautiful than any wedding."

Her eyes fill with tears. "I should go. I shouldn't even be here."

"Why didn't you just call me to tell me all this?"

She frowns. "What?"

"You could have called me but you didn't. You came here for a reason. You wanted to see me again." She opens her mouth to reply but closes it again. "What do you need from me, Lori?"

"What are you talking about?"

"You need something from me but I can't figure out what. Did you come here for closure? Do you need me to end it for good? Or is it the opposite? Do you need me to make the first move? Do you need me to remind you how good we are together?"

"I...I don't know." Her eyes turn sad. "I don't know anymore, Buzz."

"Listen to your heart."

She sighs. "It's not that simple."

"Yes, it is. What do you *want*, Lori?"

"I want it all."

I take a step closer to her. "You want it all?" She nods. "Then take it. Take what you want. Take what you need. Do what you've got to do."

"But I want different things from different people. If I take what I need, people are going to get hurt."

"And if you *don't* take what you need, people are still going to get hurt, including yourself."

We stand still, looking at each other in silence for what feels like minutes until she finally says, "I should go." My heart sinks. The most fucked up part is that I can tell she doesn't even want to leave. She glances towards my bedroom. "I'm sure there are plenty of girls who would love to warm your bed." She looks down at her feet. "I meant what I said last night. You should get it out of your system. It might help you to move on."

"You're the only one I want in there."

"We have some great memories, let's not taint them."

I take a step closer to her. "I don't want you to be a memory."

"Then maybe we could work on being friends."

"We could never be friends."

"Well that's your choice."

"No, it's not. I don't have a choice in any of this. If I had a choice, I would choose to be with you but you're choosing *him*."

"If you had a choice, you would choose me?" She shakes her head. "You had a choice six months ago and you *didn't* choose me. It's too late. You can't pick and choose when you want me, Buzz."

She goes to walk away but I pull her back to me. "I've never stopped wanting you. I thought I was doing the right thing. I knew that I wouldn't have been able to handle your job. It would have driven me crazy. I didn't want to ruin what we had."

"But you ruined what we had by breaking up with me! Why can't you see that?" She shrugs out of my grasp and walks over to the door. "We're done here."

"That's a lie and we both know it. We'll never be done, Lori. This is just another cliffhanger."

"Call it whatever you want but please stay away from John."

"Is that where you're going now? To be with him? Tell him I say hello, won't you? Oh, and when he's taking off your clothes, be sure to tell him how much they turned me on, especially your skirt." My eyes roam her body. "Tell him that when I'm jerking off tonight, I'll be thinking about you wearing that skirt and nothing else. In my head, I'll be hitching it up around your thighs, bending you over and fucking you as hard as I can."

"Stop it."

"What? I'm just being honest with you. That's what you want, right? Honesty? What's the other one you mentioned? Loyalty? I was actually planning on watching some librarian porn, but I'll stay *loyal* to you and just think about you instead."

"You're disgusting."

"Will you think about me too? Will you think about me later while he's fucking you?"

"Don't talk to me like that."

"Why? You used to love it when I talked dirty to you. Does John do it too? Hey, do you ever pretend that you're fucking me instead of him? Actually, I'm guessing it's always over too quickly for it to be believable."

"Fuck you."

"That's a great idea." I take a step closer so that our bodies are flush. "*Fuck me.* Go ahead. I'm all yours." Her eyes widen when my dick twitches against her stomach. "It's a shame you can't say the same thing back to me." I've never seen her look so pissed off and turned on at the same time. I stare at her, silently daring her to

110

make a move and desperately urging her to follow her heart.

But she doesn't.

Instead, she listens to her fears and society's shitty expectations of her and without saying a word, she throws the door open and storms outside. I watch as she marches over to a silver Porsche and climbs inside. Unless she's bought herself a new car, I'm guessing it belongs to the dentist. I glance at the registration plate and groan when sure enough I see that it's personalized.

'C12OWN'

What a pretentious asshole. I don't care if he wants to get married and have children…she still doesn't belong with him. She leans forward and presses her head against the steering wheel. I want to go out to her. Hell, I want to lie down in front of the damn car so that she can't leave. Maybe I could just slit his tires instead. She rubs the back of her neck, which she does when she's stressed, and I'd be lying if I said it doesn't make me feel better to see that she's struggling with her decision to leave.

She finally starts the engine and I force myself to close the door. There's no way I can watch her drive away knowing she's on her way back to another man.

I walk into the kitchen and calmly pour myself a glass of whiskey before downing it in one. Then I pour another. I take a few deep breaths and try to trick myself into thinking that I'm a mature adult. It lasts for all of thirty seconds before I launch the glass against the opposite side of the room. I curse as tiny shards fly in all different directions. The way I'm feeling right now, they might as well be stabbing me right through the heart.

I can't lose her.

I stare at the glass on the floor and feel a weird kind of disconnect with the world. I'm no longer a participant but a spectator, watching my life head down the wrong path.

After a couple of minutes, I begin to move around on autopilot. There's nothing I can do other than attempt to pick up the pieces, both literally and figuratively. I throw some of the bigger shards away just as I hear my neighbor pull up outside. I'm relieved she wasn't home five minutes ago because I sure as shit don't want to be the reason why an eighty-year-old lady has a heart attack. Surely my own broken heart meets the quota for the street.

I slice my finger when there's a quiet knock at my door. I stand up and suck the blood as I walk over to answer it. My stomach flips as I open the door. It's not my neighbor. It's Lori. She came back. I try not to get my hopes up. Maybe she's broken down. Maybe she left something here. *Or maybe she realized what a huge fucking mistake she was making by choosing John.* I open the door wider and her eyes turn hungry.

"Remind me," she says, referring to my earlier comment. "Remind me how good we are together."

I don't need to be told twice. I'll remind her so hard that she won't ever forget it. I close the gap between us and take her face in my hands. When I kiss her, it feels like we've never been apart. It feels right. Our hands work quickly but our tongues work even quicker. I walk backwards, pulling her with me as she kicks the door shut.

I push her up against the kitchen wall and she grabs my ass, pulling me even closer to her. She moans when my dick presses against her and I almost forgot just how much I love all the different sounds that she makes. I pull away and angle her neck to the side before sucking and biting like I'm some kind of starved cannibal. I need

112

her so bad. I'm going to explode if I can't get inside of her soon.

I rip open her blouse and she squeals as little gold buttons pop off in every direction. I stare at her lacy bra for about half a second before it joins the buttons on the floor. I take a nipple into my mouth and suck it as hard as I can while rolling the other one between my fingers. I pause but only long enough to switch to the other one. My dick throbs as a feral moan escapes her lips. I can't wait any longer. I drop to my knees and keep my eyes on hers as I slowly push her skirt up as high as it will go. After draping her leg over my shoulder, I trail gentle kisses up her thigh and when I reach her panties, I can feel just how much she wants this. I yank them to the side and she gasps as I push two fingers inside of her. I go as deep as I can and find the spot which men like John won't even know exists. I circle her clit at the same time, starting slow before increasing the pace and when her moaning gets louder and her body begins to squirm, I stop. I chuckle when she cries out in protest. "I forgot how impatient you are," I say as I get to my feet and carry her over to the kitchen counter, not giving a fuck about the broken glass on the floor.

"And I forgot how much of a tease *you* are," she replies.

I place her onto her back then pull her towards me so that her ass is on the edge. She hooks her legs around my waist and yanks me forward, positioning my dick exactly where it needs to be. I grin as I grab hold of her legs then bend down until they're wrapped around my neck instead. "If I'm a tease then I suppose I should live up to my name." She groans in frustration, but I silence her by kissing her wet pussy. She threads her hands through my hair and begins to move against my mouth as my tongue flicks up and down her opening. I take it slow, savoring the taste of her and wishing that this moment could last forever. I alternate between sucking her clit and fucking her with my tongue and it's not too long until she's teetering on the edge.

"Please, Buzz," she moans.

"Please what?" I ask, grinning.

"Make me come."

My dick throbs when she says my three favorite words of all time. "Oh, I intend to, but you have an important decision to make first."

She continues to desperately ride my face. "Please," she begs. "I'm so close."

I pull away. "I know you are. Tell me…do you want to come on my face or around my dick?"

"Dick. Now."

That's the answer I was hoping for. I unwrap her legs from around my neck and stand up, pulling her into a sitting position. I press my mouth against hers and use my tongue to part her lips. "Can you taste that?" I ask. "Can you taste what I do to you?"

"Yes," she replies, her eyes full of pained desire.

I pull my pants and boxers down and then kick them off so that I'm completely naked. She looks at my dick and her eyes go wide like it's the first time she's seeing it. "What's up, sweetheart? Did you forget how big it was?"

She rolls her eyes. "Actually, it's smaller than I remember. Now please hurry up."

I laugh. "Hmmm, maybe I should make you wait a little longer?" I grab my dick and start to move up and down. "We should probably wait until it's *bigger*." I would rip her to shreds if I was any bigger, but I can't resist teasing her.

She jumps down off the counter and pushes my hand away. My head falls back as she takes over but I'm way too horny for a hand job. The only way I'm going to be satisfied is by being inside of her. She squeals as I quickly turn her around and bend her over. I push her skirt up even further then grab onto an ass cheek as I position my dick. I tease her with the tip, moving it up and down until she gets impatient and moves her ass back, pushing me deep inside of her. She gasps as I start to move, nice and slow to begin with. If this doesn't remind her how good we are together, I don't know what will. She lifts her ass even higher as she lets her arms drop, pressing the side of her face against the counter. I grab the back of her hair, which doesn't even resemble a bun anymore and increase the pace. She cries out as I pound into her, making up for lost time. I pull her head back so I can look her in the eyes and when her moaning gets louder, I pull out. She groans as I turn her around to face me. "I'm sorry but I've waited six months to watch you come again."

Her eyes are two dark slits. "Then watch me."

I lift her back up onto the counter and she wraps her legs around me. "I need to hear you say my name."

I thrust into her without warning and she cries out, pulling me even closer to her. "Oh, Buzz!"

"That's it, baby. Say my name."

"Oh, fuck. Keep going. That's it. Oh, Buzz! Oh, Buzz! Oh, Buzz!"

She comes long and hard and about a minute later, so do I. I look her in the eye as her body shudders. This has always been my favorite part; being so vulnerable when I'm used to having my guard up. Her head flops onto my shoulder and I pull her even closer to me, wishing that we could stay like this forever. "I've missed you," I whisper into her hair.

"I've missed you, too," she replies after a long pause.

We stay like that for a little while and when she pulls away, I see the unmistakable sadness and worry in her eyes. "Oh no, was it that bad?" I joke. "I know I'm a little rusty, but I thought I did okay."

"I'm sorry," she says as she awkwardly lifts herself off me. "My head is all messed up."

"You don't need to apologize for anything," I say as I step into my pants and pick up her bra. "We're in this together." She jumps down from the counter then pulls her skirt down, smoothing it out as best she can. My dick already misses her and is ready to go again at the sight of her wearing nothing but her skirt and heels. She takes the bra out of my hand and puts it back on while looking around for her blouse. I bend down to pick it up then shake it to make sure there's no glass on it. "I'm sorry I ruined it," I say with a smirk. "I'll buy you another one."

She shakes her head as she slips back into it. "It's fine."

"Do you want to wear one of my shirts instead?"

"No," she replies a little too quickly. "No. I've got a jacket in the car."

"I think you should forget about the blouse and just wear the skirt. It's a good look on you. I knew it would be. My imagination never fails me." I pull her into my arms

116

and thread my hands through hers. "Have you eaten? Do you want to order takeout? I've worked up an appetite."

She grimaces and pulls away from me. "Um, no. I need to get back."

"What? You're leaving already?"

"John doesn't know where I am and I've got his car. He's probably getting worried."

"Well how about I come with you? We can return the car then come back here or go to your place, whichever you'd prefer."

She shakes her head as her eyes fill with tears. "I tried to leave, Buzz. I *wanted* to leave but it was like some kind of thread was pulling me back to you. I got stopped at about five red lights in a row and I thought it was a sign. I needed to be with you one last time."

My heart sinks and a shiver runs down my spine. "One last time?"

"It was selfish of me. I'm sorry."

"Wait…are you going back to him?"

"Buzz…"

"Oh, wow. You're actually going back to him, aren't you? After what we just did?"

"Please. I don't know what I can say to make any of this better. This whole situation is fucked up."

"No. What's fucked up is that you're going home to another man while my come is still inside you." Her face falls. "Did that mean nothing to you? Was it just a quick fuck?"

"Please don't do this. You know that's not what it was."

"No, I *don't* know. I don't have a clue what's happening. You came here tonight and reeled off a list of reasons why you can't be with me but then you came back here and practically begged me to fuck you. Forgive me for not being able to keep up."

A tear falls from her eye. "I'm sorry. I shouldn't have come back. This isn't fair on anybody."

I shrug, trying to act like I don't care. "Stop apologizing. I finally got laid after six months. At least I don't have to jerk…"

Her cell rings, interrupting me mid-sentence. She reaches into her purse, which I didn't even know she had, and glances at the screen. She bites her lip and cancels the call. I laugh even though there's nothing remotely funny about this situation. "Was that him?" She nods. "Well you better run back home to him. I'm guessing you're not going to tell him about what we just did?"

She looks down at her feet. "No. I don't want to hurt him."

"So you don't want to hurt *him* but you're fine with hurting *me*?"

"That's not what I meant. He doesn't need to know about it because it's never going to happen again. We both need time to move on from this so I think it'll be easier if you don't call me."

In the past, this would have been the perfect hook up but not now. Not with Lori. It's the complete opposite of what I want to hear. "Don't call you? So we're not even allowed to be friends now?"

"We could never be friends, you even said it yourself."

"So what happens now?" I ask.

"Nothing. We move on and pretend that it never happened."

"I can't do that."

"Please try."

"It's impossible to move on from you, Lori. Was that closure for you? Is that what it was?"

"Maybe. I don't even know."

"Or did you just want an orgasm? Can he not make you come?"

"Don't do this."

"Do what?" I shout. "Don't feel anything for you after what just happened?"

"You should be used to it by now."

"Used to what?"

"Fucking girls then moving on with your life. Fucking without feelings."

"Don't do that. Don't use my past against me. That's not who I am anymore, and you know it. I changed the moment that I met you. Don't try and convince yourself that I'll be okay just to make yourself feel better. When you fall asleep tonight and every other night for that matter, just know that I'm aching for you. Know that it kills me to think about you in his arms when you belong in mine."

Her tears are falling fast now. "I'm so sorry. Please don't hate me."

"Just leave. Go home to your boyfriend."

"Buzz…"

I turn away from her. I can't watch her leave, not for a second time. "Go."

I fall to my knees when I hear the door open and close. It would be easy to hate her right now. It would be easy to hate myself. Hating somebody is easy but loving somebody is the hard part. Love takes courage and now more than ever, I need to be strong. She might have lost her way, just like I did six months ago, but I won't give up on her. Nothing worth having comes easy.

CHAPTER FIFTEEN

The next morning, I feel jet lagged and hungover at the same time. That's what happens when you spend all night thinking instead of sleeping. I probably got around three hours sleep at most and those three hours were filled with dreams of Lori. No, not dreams. *Nightmares.* Nightmares about her and John being happy together. The one which hurt the most was when she left him and came back to me. It was so realistic; I could feel her in my arms. And then I woke up and it hurt all over again. I was too scared to fall back to sleep so I stayed awake and watched crappy shopping channels. I'm now the proud owner of a twirling spaghetti fork and a heated throw which also doubles up as a dressing gown. *Every cloud has a silver lining.*

After showering and forcing myself to eat a protein bar, I decide that I need to get out of the house before I drive myself crazy. I call Mason when it finally starts to get light outside.

"Hello?" he answers, sounding half-asleep.

"Coffee?"

"Buzz…it's six thirty."

"Exactly. It's the perfect time to have coffee."

He groans. "It's the worst time to have coffee."

"Why? You sound tired. Coffee will help with that."

"I *am* tired. It's six thirty on a Saturday. Sane people don't get up this early unless they have to. I'll skip the coffee but thanks for the offer…and the wake-up call."

"Anytime. Hey, is Sophia there?"

"Yeah. Why?"

"Is she in bed with you?"

"Yes..."

"Is she naked?"

He hangs up without saying bye.

I hesitate before making the next call. I know that it's going to lead to a difficult conversation, but I need to hear what she has to say. I take a deep breath and prepare myself to hear some home truths.

"Hello," she answers immediately.

"Hi, Mom."

"Why are you awake so early? You're never up at this time on a Saturday. Are you calling me from a jail cell?"

I laugh. "No, Mom, I'm not in jail. I couldn't sleep."

"Me neither and now I know why."

"Huh?"

"Mother's intuition. I must have been able to sense that you were awake."

"Um, sure. Do you want to meet up for breakfast?"

"Could we do lunch instead, sweetheart? I have a meeting with my accountant this morning."

"Of course. One o'clock at our usual spot?"

"Sounds great. See you then. Oh, and make sure you wear some pants which actually cover your butt. I'll never understand why people think it's cool to show off their underwear. What's that singer called? Justin Beaver?"

I burst out laughing. "Justin *Bieber*."

"Yes, that's the one. He's always got his underpants on show."

"And how would you know? Have you been insta-stalking him?"

"Instant what?"

"Never mind."

"Surely he can afford a pair of jeans which actually fit him. Imagine if women walked around showing their panties off?"

"Yes, I *can* imagine that...vividly. That sounds like the perfect world, Mom."

She tuts. "And while I'm on the subject of fashion, don't wear any of those skinny jeans either.

122

They're just as bad as the baggy ones. You're so tall, they make your legs look like drainpipes."

"No jeans. Anything else?"

"No, I think that's it for now."

I chuckle as I end the call. I can always count on my mom to say it exactly how it is.

I walk into the restaurant ten minutes early to make sure I can grab us a nice table, but my mom's already beat me to it. She's sitting next to the window and is deep in conversation with another woman who I've never seen before.

I make my way over to them, willing my baggy jeans to fall even further down my ass. She stands and waves when she notices me, but her smile is quickly replaced by a raised eyebrow. I don't know why she's surprised. She should know me by now. I smirk as I stop in front of her and kiss her on the cheek. "You're looking lovely today, Mother."

"That's because my clothes actually fit me," she whispers and then gestures to the woman sitting opposite her. "This is my friend Julie from college. We haven't seen each other in years. We thought it might be nice for us all to share a table."

I smile politely even though I was looking forward to some time alone with her. "Nice to meet you, Julie."

"You too. I've heard a lot about you over the years."

"Oh, I'm sure you've heard some delightful stories," I say as I sit down next to my mom. "Whatever trouble I was in, you'll be pleased to know that I've matured a lot since then."

"Have you?" my mom jokes.

Julie laughs. "I have a son a few years older than you. We used to compare notes when you were kids. You were both so cheeky. I'm sure you would have been the best of friends. I'm actually waiting to meet him and my daughter-in-law for lunch." She giggles to herself. "Look at me getting carried away. She's not my daughter-in-law yet but I'm sure she will be soon. My son is extremely smitten by her. He's already mentioned ring shopping. It's all so exciting! I've been out of town so this is the first time I'm meeting her. We've spoken on FaceTime but it's not the same, is it?"

"Is it your Sebastian?" my mom asks.

"No, not Seb. It's my youngest, Jonathan. Oh look, here they come right now."

My blood runs cold when I look over at the door and see Lori and John walking towards us, hand in hand. John is her son? This can't be happening. I must be dreaming. This is just another nightmare. *Wake up, Buzz.* I pinch myself but nothing happens.

John spots me first. His eyes widen then quickly narrow as he whispers something to Lori, who is looking down at her feet. Her head immediately snaps up and our eyes lock. Everything turns to slow motion as I'm transported back to last night when she was mine. She looks confused as she slows her walk and whispers something back to him. A different emotion flashes in her eyes and I'm pretty sure it's relief. I cling to it like my life depends on it.

Julie stands up. "Jonathan! Lori! I'm so happy you're here." She wraps her arms around Lori. "It's so great to finally meet you!"

Lori smiles politely. Even though she could give Jennifer Lawrence a run for her money, I can tell that deep down she's feeling just as awkward as I am. "You too, Mrs Crown."

"Please call me Julie. Before we get to anything else, I want to thank you for making my son so happy."

Dagger, meet heart.

My mom's hand finds mine under the table and she gives it a little squeeze. I turn to face her and she nods

124

reassuringly, her eyes full of understanding. Has her mother's intuition kicked in again? Can she sense how much I'm hurting right now? I never told her why I broke up with Lori, but she saw how happy we were together…and how *unhappy* I was after we split. Lori is the only woman that I have *ever* taken home to meet my mom.

"John, Lori, this is my old friend from college and her son."

My mom smiles. "Nice to meet you, John. And I've already had the pleasure of meeting Lori."

"Oh, really?" Julie asks. "What a small world! How do you two know each other?"

This should be interesting.

"We have the same friends," Lori quickly replies.

"My best friend is engaged to Lori's best friend," I add.

"Aww, how sweet! When are they getting married?"

I roll my eyes when John pulls a chair out for his mom and then for Lori. Why does he try so hard to be perfect? Perfect is overrated.

"Next spring," Lori says as she pours herself a glass of water. My eyes fall to her mouth and I watch as she takes a little sip. Memories of last night come flooding back and I picture my name falling from her lips over and over again as I made her come. *Awesome.* As if getting a hard-on in front of my mother isn't bad enough, I'm also sitting opposite my ex, her new boyfriend and his mother. My life is getting more and more fucked up by the second.

Julie wiggles her eyebrows up and down. "A spring wedding sounds perfect, doesn't it, John?"

He laughs. "Yes. A summer wedding sounds pretty perfect too. Or a fall wedding. Or even a winter one. Which season would you like to get married in, babe?"

I wait for her to say winter.

"I don't think it really matters," she replies, looking like she wants the ground to open up and swallow her. "But I've always liked the thought of a winter wedding."

Bingo.

"Me too," John says with a wink. *Prick.* I grab on to the edge of the table when he adds. "A winter wedding it'll be then."

"Oh," my mom says. "I didn't realize you were wedding planning."

"We're not" Lori says, looking from my mom to me. I'm pleased by her answer until she adds, "Not yet."

"There's no need to rush into anything," I say. "You should take your time…consider all of your options."

"Oh, I think Lori knows what she wants by now," John replies, taking hold of her hand.

She certainly knew what she wanted last night and it wasn't dentist dick.

"Haven't you always said that you wanted to be married by the time you were thirty, babe?"

My mum clears her throat. "For years I always said that I never wanted children but look at me now, sitting next to my son who just so happens to be the most extraordinary person I know." I want to give her a high five as I watch John's smug little smile disappear from his face. "People can change their minds. Life is about the journey, not the destination."

"Indeed," John replies. "But it's always sensible to have a destination in mind, right? Otherwise we may never get to where we want to be."

"If you want to be somewhere bad enough, you'll arrive when the time is right. What is meant for you will not pass you."

I squeeze my mom's hand under the table then glance at Lori. Her head is tilted to one side as though she's thinking carefully about what my mom just said. We all sit in silence for a few seconds before Julie laughs. "Look at us being all serious. I'm guessing you don't believe in marriage then, Buzz?"

"I believe that loving someone for the rest of your life should be enough. I don't understand why a piece of paper holds more weight than a person's word. But saying that, if it was the only way I could be with the woman I loved then I would get married right here, right now."

"I'm sure that woman wouldn't want you to get married just because it was the *only* way to keep her," John chips in.

"Oh, I'm sure she would appreciate the fact that I would do anything for her. I won't stop fighting for her."

"Your view on it sounds a little unhealthy to me."

"Unhealthy? Hmmm. Would you say it's more or less unhealthy than printing off somebody's photo without them knowing, framing it and then displaying it on their desk at work?"

Lori almost chokes on her drink and then stands up. "Excuse me. I need to use the restroom."

My mom stands up too, probably sensing that I was about to go after her. "I'll go with you."

I look from John to his mother. Well isn't this cozy?

"I think it's lovely that you would do anything for the woman that you love," Julie says which is followed by a look of disgust from John.

"Thank you, Julie," I reply, smugly. "I hope you'll excuse me, too. I just need to make a quick phone call."

I walk outside and count to ten in my head, wondering how long it'll take for John to join me.

One. Two. Three. Four. Five. Si...

The door opens.

I fold my arms across my chest as he heads in my direction. "Why are you here?" he asks, getting straight to the point.

"The same reason as you."

127

"You're here to introduce Lori to your mother?"

"Nah, Lori has already been introduced to my mother. They get along really well, actually."

"Then we're not here for the same reason. Why are you doing this?"

I sigh. "Believe it or not, I didn't know you were going to be here today. I came to have lunch with my mom."

"I don't believe you."

"I don't care."

He looks deep in thought and after a long pause asks me, "Where were you last night?"

I can't hide my smirk. I know that what we did was wrong, but the guy is a total asshole. "I was at home."

"Doing what?"

"Lots of things."

"Did you happen to see Lori?"

"Why would I have seen Lori?"

"Because she went missing for a couple of hours."

"Did you file a missing persons report?"

"Funny."

"Did you try asking her where she was?"

"She said she was at a friend's house."

"Then she was at a friend's house. What's the matter, don't you trust her?"

"I do trust her."

"Then what's the problem?"

"I don't trust *you*. You're my problem."

I laugh. "You don't even know me."

"I know enough about you. She came home in a weird mood."

"And why do you think it has anything to do with me?"

"Because everything was going great until we had dinner with you a couple of nights ago. Since then, she's been trapped inside of her own head. It's like a wall has come up. She's become distant."

"Then you need to talk to her about it, not me."

"I've tried. She refuses to talk about you. It's like you're that Voldemord guy and I'm not even allowed to mention your name."

"It's *Voldemort* and I'm pretty sure she would break up with you right now if she heard you calling him that." *So go ahead, keep on saying it.*

"What happened between you two? What did you do to her?"

"What did I *do* to her? Are you being serious right now?"

"Yes, I am. You must have done something. Did you cheat on her?"

"Fuck you." I can feel my blood bubbling underneath my skin. "I would never cheat on her," I tell him through clenched teeth.

"Then what happened?"

"It's none of your goddamn business."

He smirks and nods his head. "So you *did* cheat on her."

I take a step closer to him. "I didn't cheat on her and if I have to tell you again, I'm not going to be happy about it."

"What are you going to do? Stop by my office and damage more of my stuff?"

"No, I'll damage your fucking face."

"No wonder she's with me now instead of you. She had a lucky escape."

I can't decide if he's brave or stupid but I'm about to find out. I close the gap between us and peer down at him. "Say that again." The only thing I can think about is how much I would love to knock him out. It's a good thing my mom and Lori are here otherwise I would have already done it by now.

I hear the door open but I don't take my eyes off John until Lori appears next to him, looking worried. "Buzz," she says quietly, and I'd be lying if I said it didn't

129

feel good that she's concentrating on me instead of him. "What's going on?" she asks.

"Nothing," John answers for me as he takes a couple of steps back. "I was just getting some air."

"And quizzing me on what I was doing last night," I add. "Apparently you went missing for a couple of hours and he seems to think that I know where you were." Her face turns even paler. "I can't speak for John, but I want you to know that *I* trust you. I trust your judgement. So wherever you were last night and whatever you were doing, I trust that you made the right decision at that time. I believe that you were exactly where you needed to be."

She looks at me with so much raw emotion in her eyes that I can't imagine what it must feel like to be John right now. How can he be okay with his girlfriend looking at another man like that?

Apparently he's not okay with it as he narrows his eyes and steps in between me and Lori. "You know that I trust you," he tells her. "I just got a little protective over my girl, that's all." *His girl?* I deserve a fucking medal for not losing my shit. "It's only because I care about you so much," he continues. He *cares* about her? I care about my grandma. I care about what toppings I have on my pizza. Saying that I care for Lori would be a huge insult. What I feel for her is way more meaningful than that. "It won't happen again, babe." He turns and holds out his right hand to me. "I'm sorry for involving you. I realize that you're insignificant and have nothing to do with our relationship. You're her past but I'm her future."

I laugh at his fake, passive-aggressive apology but shake his hand, squeezing it as hard as I can. Super mature of me, I know. He tries his best to hide the pain and I hope he feels it all day long. "Let's get back inside," he tells her when I finally let go.

She glances at me. "I'm sorry."

"For what exactly?"

"Everything." She lowers her voice. "Everything that's happened and everything that might happen."

"I'm not sure what that even means."

"Come on, babe," John says as he starts to back away, holding his hand out.

"Do you regret it?" I whisper so that only she can hear me. Her eyes fill with sadness. "I'm guessing that means you do."

She looks over her shoulder at John, checking that he can't hear her as she says, "It means that I don't." My heart swells and breaks at the same time as I watch her walk back inside with him.

I'm still staring at the door a few minutes later when my mom walks out. "Hi, Son." She leans her head against my shoulder. "Are you okay?"

"Not really."

"Of course you're not. Why didn't you tell me that she was with someone else?"

"I only found out a couple of days ago."

"Well I'm here for you. What do you need?"

"I need *her*." She sighs and begins to fiddle with her necklace. "How was she?" I ask. "Did you speak to her?"

She nods. "This is hard for her, son."

"Hard for *her*?"

"Yes."

"Then how does she think *I'm* feeling?"

"I'm pretty sure she has enough on her plate without having to worry about how you're feeling too. You may spend your nights alone, but she spends her nights battling her head and her heart. And while you're in love with somebody you can't have, she's in love with two people."

"She told you that?"

"She didn't need to tell me. It's about empathy, darling. This isn't easy for anybody involved. This is a turning point for her. She's not just deciding who she wants to be with. She's figuring out who she is and she's trying to make a decision which she knows will probably affect her for the next fifty years of her life. So yes, this is hard for *her*."

I sigh. "I can't watch her marry him, mom."

"You might have to." Hearing the truth crushes me. Why is it so hard to breathe all of a sudden? "If you're meant to end up together then you'll end up together. It's as simple as that. You have to be on the same page at the same time. If you expect her to be patient with you and your views on marriage and commitment, then you need to be patient with her in return. If marrying John is part of her story, then you need to let her write it. That's the hardest part about this thing that we call life. Nobody can predict the future. You just have to keep the love in your heart and pray that your happy ending is with Lori." She nudges me. "Life is pretty damn wonderful too. We get to edit when we want to. If we don't like something, we can rip out a page or even a whole chapter. John is a part of Lori's story, but he isn't the whole book."

"Can't we just skip ahead to the chapter where we get back together again?"

She smiles. "I wish you could.

I wrap an arm around her shoulders. "We better get back inside. I don't want Julie to think that we're being rude."

"I've already taken care of it. Let's go and get some ice cream."

I laugh. "I'm not a kid anymore, mom. You don't have to take me for ice cream."

"But it never fails to cheer you up. Besides, I'm not taking you. *You're* taking *me*."

CHAPTER SIXTEEN

Mason calls just as I'm finishing up eating my ice cream. My mom was right. Even though my heart is craving Lori, my soul was craving mint choc chip. I'm already feeling a little bit better, or at least not as bad. I'm pretty sure it has more to do with my mom's pep talk than the ice cream though. "Look who's finally awake," I say in greeting.

"*Finally* awake? I was awake at six thirty thanks to you," he replies.

"Then why didn't you come for coffee?"

"Because I wanted to stay in bed with my beautiful fiancée." I make the sound of a whip cracking. "Hey! Don't act like you wouldn't do the same. When you were with Lori, I wouldn't hear from you for entire weekends at a time. You used to forget that anybody else existed." *Used to?* "Where are you anyway?" he asks. "Is that a kid crying?"

I look over at the little boy who is acting like the world is about to end. Welcome to the club, kid. "Yeah, he's just dropped his ice cream."

"Ice cream? Where are you?"

"Delucci's."

"Why are you there?"

"Why *wouldn't* I be here? Not everybody is allergic to ice cream like you are."

"Oh yeah, I forgot that most people can eat it without *dying*. What are you really doing there?"

"I'm cheering myself up."

"You're making me work for my answers today. Why do you need cheering up?"

I sigh dramatically. "Because my best friend wouldn't come for coffee with me."

"Wow, you really want to make me feel bad about it, huh? Come on, stop messing. Who are you there with?"

"My mom."

"Oh. Well make sure you tell her I said thanks for last night."

"I don't have to, you're on loud speaker."

He starts to choke and then whispers, "Shit. Are you being serious?"

I chuckle. "No, I'm joking."

"Thank god for that."

"But don't worry, I'll tell her now."

"Buzz…"

"Mom," I shout but not loud enough for her to hear. "Mason says thanks for last night." He curses on the other end of the line. "What's wrong?" I ask innocently. "You wanted me to tell her."

"You're fired."

"And you're full of shit. I've heard that about five hundred times. Come up with a new threat."

He sighs. "Let me talk to your mom."

"She's busy entertaining the crying toddler. She's a sucker for kids."

"Wait. So she isn't even with you?"

"Nope."

"You son of a bitch! I was going to invite you to my house for a few games of pool, but you can forget about it now."

"When? Tonight?"

"Yeah. Sophia's going out for dinner. We could order take-out."

"Sounds good. I'll be there around seven."

"See you then. Tell your mom to call me."

"Mom," I shout again but this time she turns around. "Mason wants you to call him."

"Okay, darling," she replies.

Mason groans. "I hate you."

"I love you too, Brother."

CHAPTER SEVENTEEN

"You're a cheating bastard."

"How did I cheat?" Mason asks.

"You moved the ball when I wasn't looking."

"No, I didn't. You're just a sore loser."

He's right but I'll never admit it. "Rematch?"

"That *was* the rematch."

"Best of three?"

He laughs. "As long as you're okay with losing again, cry baby. I'm sure there are some tissues lying around here somewhere."

"You carry a pack in your pocket, remember? For when you're always jerking off."

He laughs. "I'm engaged, *remember?* You're the one who needs them." I've always had a terrible poker face and today is no different. He tilts his head to the side. "Of course you don't need them. Who was it this time?"

I simply shrug. I want to confide in him but after the day I've had, I'm not in the mood for a lecture. I already know what he's going to say. Sometimes it's hard being best friends with Mr Perfect. I'm always going to look like a fuck-up compared to him. "It doesn't matter."

"Does that mean you can't remember her name? Or did you not even bother to ask?"

"No. It means it doesn't matter." I collect the balls and begin to rack them when I hear the front door close, followed by voices. I look at my cell. "Sophia's back early," I say to Mason, changing the subject. "I thought you said she only left ten minutes before I got here."

He frowns. "Yeah, she did. That's weird."

I follow him towards the hallway and both my legs and heart forget how to function when I see Lori standing behind Sophia. They're deep in conversation but fall silent when they notice us. Lori's eyes widen but Sophia's narrow. "What are you doing here?" she asks.

I chuckle. "It's nice to see you too, Soph."

She gives Mason a fake smile. "You didn't mention that Buzz was stopping by."

"I didn't realize I had to." He winks at her. "Why are you back so early?"

"The, um, restaurant…it was fully booked."

I can tell that she's lying by the way Lori is shifting from one foot to the other. My chin tilts up in question but she answers with a small shake of her head.

"Never mind," Mason says, unaware of our little exchange. "You can have take-out with us instead. Buzz ordered enough food to feed a small village."

"I ordered three pizzas," I correct him.

"For two people. Plus the chicken wings and fries."

Sophia turns to Lori and gives her a pointed look. "I'm not sure what we're doing yet. Are we going back out? We could try a different restaurant."

"No, it's fine," she replies.

Sophia raises an eyebrow. "Are you sure?"

"Like Mason said, there's enough food for everyone," I add.

"Well she might not want what you're offering."

Lori places a hand on her arm, "Soph, it's fine."

"Yeah, Soph, it's fine," I say. "She will definitely want what I'm offering. It's extremely satisfying and very filling."

Sensing the weird atmosphere, Mason taps me on the shoulder. "Come on. I need to beat you at pool."

"You already beat me," I say, reluctant to leave Lori.

"You asked for best of three, remember?"

There's no chance in hell that I'm going to play pool while Lori is in the same building as me. I want to spend every minute I can get with her, especially while the dickhead dentist isn't here. "It's fine," I tell him. "You won fair and square."

He feigns shock. "Can I have that in writing?"

I hold up my middle finger. "You can have *this* in writing."

He laughs. "You three go and sit down, I'll get us some drinks."

"No, I'll get them," Sophia says. "Lori wants to see your game room."

"I do?" she asks, looking confused.

"Yes, you do. Buzz can help me with the drinks." Lori rolls her eyes but Sophia simply waves her away and gestures for me to follow her into the kitchen.

"Can we have beer instead of that posh crap you had the other night?" I ask as the door closes behind us.

She ignores me and opens the utensil drawer. "Take a long, hard look at all of those knives, Buzz."

"Um, okay?"

"Don't make me use one on you."

I hold my hands up. "Woah, woah, woah! What are you talking about?"

She slams the drawer shut and lowers her voice. "I know what you did."

I look around. "Are we filming some kind of crappy horror movie?"

"We can be. I've just shown you my knives." She narrows her eyes and points at me. "You promised to leave them alone."

"Oh, is this about Lori?"

"Of course it's about Lori. She told me what happened last night."

I shrug. "Shit happens."

"Shit happens?" She takes a step closer to me. "You know that I like you but don't you dare mess around with my best friend. We had to leave the restaurant because she couldn't stop crying!"

My heart sinks. "She's upset?"

"Of course she's upset! She's riddled with guilt and her head is all over the place. Lori isn't a cheater but what you did has turned her into one. Why did you do it? To piss off John?"

I begin to pace up and down. "This has nothing to do with him."

"Then why?"

"Because I still have feelings for her. I thought you would understand after our conversation the other night."

"And *I* thought you were going to give her some space to see what happened with John, not jump into bed with her less than twenty four hours later!"

"We didn't make it to my bed."

She throws her hands up in the air. "One minute she's talking about moving in with John and the next minute she's talking about leaving him!"

My heart leaps out of my fucking chest. "Wait...she's leaving him?"

"No! Maybe! Ugh, I don't know!"

"Well what did she say? Is she seriously considering leaving him?"

"We're not having this conversation. I've already said too much."

"Fine, I'll have it with Lori instead…"

"Don't you dare! I'm only telling you because you need to know how confused she is. She's vulnerable at the minute and you should give her some space to sort her shit out."

"It's not fair that you're asking me to stay away. Her decision will affect me too."

"I just don't want you to make this harder on her."

"I was trying to make it easier for her. I was trying to remind her how good we are together and by the sounds of it, it seems to have worked."

"She's good with John too."

"Whose side are you on?"

"Lori's," she simply replies, hands on hips, looking like she's ready for battle.

"Me too."

"No. You're on your own side."

"If I was on my own side, I'd be fucking anything with a heartbeat. I'd be sleeping like a baby instead of staying awake all night thinking about her. Trust me when I say that I'm doing neither of those things."

She sighs as she walks over to the fridge, pulling out several cans of beer and passing them to me. "Please don't hurt her. I was left to pick up the pieces six months ago and I don't want to do it all over again."

"You won't have to." I just hope that it's a two-way street. "Have you finished threatening me?"

"Threatening you? Trust me…that was just a friendly warning."

"Jesus Christ. Mason's got his hands full. Thank god I chose Lori instead."

She scowls and pushes me towards the door. "Get out of my kitchen."

"With pleasure," I mumble under my breath.

"I heard that!" she shouts just as the door is closing behind me.

I head towards the lounge and place the beers down in front of Mason who is scrolling through Netflix.

"Netflix and chill?" I ask.

"How many times do I have to tell you? I'm engaged…and straight."

"You're not my type anyway."

He chuckles. "Then who is?"

"Chris Hemsworth."

"*Thor*?"

"Yep. Rough and rugged."

He bursts out laughing. "You want Thor's hammer?"

"Yeah to play whack-a-mole on your head. Where's Lori?"

"What about his brother Liam? You could have a threesome."

"Nah, he's too clean cut. Where's Lori?"

"Wait a minute…so you like dirty old men with big hammers?"

I ignore him and walk out of the room to the sound of him laughing.

I head straight for the game room and sure enough find Lori perched on the edge of the pool table, looking at Mason's artwork. She gives me a sad smile when she sees me. "Hi," I say as I sit down next to her.

"Hi," she replies.

"What do you think?" I ask, gesturing to the canvas.

"I don't get it."

"If you squint, it kind of looks like a horse riding on a cloud."

I laugh when she actually squints. "Hmmm, it looks more like a cow standing on the top of a mountain to me."

We sit in silence for at least a minute. "How are you?" I whisper.

"Not great. You?"

"Fucking miserable."

Her chin drops to her chest. "Has Sophia just threatened to chop off your balls?"

"Pretty much."

She grimaces. "I'm sorry."

"It's fine. I get it."

"I just needed to talk to somebody about it."

"You can always talk to me."

She shakes her head. "I needed to talk to somebody impartial."

"Impartial? She's your best friend."

She laughs and it's like music to my ears. "You know what I'm saying. Somebody who isn't directly involved. I have a feeling your advice would be a little biased."

"Biased? Never. I'd tell you the truth…which is that you should break up with John immediately."

"Oh, really?"

"Yep."

"And why do you think that?"

Because he's a fucking idiot. "How long have we got? This could take a while."

She rolls her eyes. "I'm listening."

"Number one – he's a dentist. You must feel pressured to have fresh breath all of the time."

"No, not really."

"Well you should. I know how much you love garlic. Number two – he's five foot two."

"He's five nine."

"Hey, does he need one of those toddler steps to reach the sink?"

"Stop it."

"Okay. Serious question now. When you wear heels, does he just disappear? Do you have to crouch down and look for him?"

"Not everybody can be a giant like you."

"You're right, they can't. Which leads me to my next point - he has a tiny dick."

She raises an eyebrow. "Says who?"

"I'm only saying what you're thinking. You're not exactly in a rush to deny it." She scowls but keeps quiet. "You're *still* not denying it which must mean that I'm right. You shouldn't settle for a teenie weenie." I grab my crotch. "Especially when you can have this."

"I'm not discussing the size of his penis with you."

"Fair enough. Number four…"

"Oh, you still haven't finished?"

"Nope. Number four – he keeps a lock of your hair on his desk at work."

"What the hell are you talking about?

143

"You know, next to his framed Facebook photograph of you."

"Oh, you must mean the one you threw in the bin."

"That's the one. The one which I took of you when you were in my bed…naked."

"Yes, you keep reminding me of that fact. Anything else?"

I slide off the edge of the table and stand directly in front of her. "Yes," I reply, no longer joking around. "He's not me."

We stare at each other for a long time and I can't remember the last time I took a breath. The air shifts, becoming so thick that I can't see anything but her and the hungry look in her eyes. I have no doubt that she wants me just as much as I want her.

She uncrosses her legs and her dress rides up, revealing smooth, toned thighs. I have to fight the urge to wrap them around my neck like I did last night. I place my hands down on either side of her and take a step closer. "Buzz…" she warns as my thighs press up against her bare knees.

"If you were mine," I tell her. "I would fuck you right here on this pool table." A tiny moan escapes her lips. "You'd like that, wouldn't you?"

"Buzz, we can't do this."

"You mean we can't even *talk* about fucking?"

"Last night was…"

"Fucking awesome?" I interrupt.

"A mistake."

"Making mistakes has to be better than faking perfections…or you know, orgasms."

She rolls her eyes. "That doesn't justify making the mistake in the first place. What we did was wrong."

"How can it be wrong when it felt so right?" I lean in even closer. "Do you need me to remind you how good it felt? How *right* it felt?"

"No. It was a one-time thing, Buzz. I can't do it again."

"You can do whatever the hell you want. *Whoever* you want."

She closes her eyes. "Please stop making it so damn hard to resist you."

"Please stop *trying* so hard to resist me," I shoot back.

I'm not sure which open first – her eyes or her legs but it doesn't matter. All that matters is that my mouth is on hers.

And her tongue is caressing mine.

And my hand is gripping the back of her neck.

And she's fisting my t-shirt, pulling me closer.

And my rock-hard dick is pressing into her.

And she's wrapping her legs around me.

And Sophia is shouting.

Wait…

"What the hell are you doing?" she shouts from the door as she rushes over to us. "No, no, no! Get off the fucking table." I take a step back and help Lori down. "I leave you alone for two minutes and this is how I find you! Jesus Christ! You are *not* using my house as your little sordid love nest."

"I'm sorry," Lori mumbles.

"You know that I love you both and I love you even more as a couple but you're with John now. Until you break up with him, I don't approve of what you're doing. I don't like it and I certainly won't be a part of it. So you can either go home and take your bad karma with you or stay here and keep your dirty little hands off each other."

I salute her. "Yes, Mom."

"Go and eat your damn pizza," she tells me. "It arrived a couple of minutes ago."

I turn to Lori. "Are you okay?" She nods, still breathing heavily. "I'll save you some of the pepperoni." I leave the room but stop just outside the doorway where I'm out of sight.

"What were you thinking?" I hear Sophia whisper angrily.

"I *wasn't* thinking" she answers.

"You can't drop your panties every time he flashes a smile at you, Lor."

Why not?

"I have no self-control around him."

"Well yeah, that's becoming blatantly obvious."

"It's like I'm a completely different person to who I was a few days ago. Seeing him has brought back all these emotions that I worked hard to bury. I think I'm addicted to him."

"Addictions are dangerous," Sophia replies.

"I'm not sure how to quit him."

Don't quit me.

"But you want to? Quit him?"

Please don't quit me.

"No, I don't think I do." She sighs. "But I know what's best for me."

"And that's John?"

My heart stops as I wait for her to answer. "Yes." My whole body deflates. "I know that my heart would be safe with him, but I don't want to live with any regrets, you know? I don't want Buzz to be the one that got away. What I have with him is pretty special. I'm not sure I'll find that with anybody else, not even with John. I told Buzz that I want the white picket fence but what good is it if you're constantly wondering if the grass is greener on the other side of it?"

"But you've been on the other side. You already know whether it's greener."

"I can't compare them. They're like night and day. I think that's why it's so difficult."

"Well you need to figure out what you want ASAP. It's cruel to lead them on."

146

I jump when somebody taps me on the shoulder. I wheel around to see Mason, his eyebrow raised. "Are you spying on my fiancée again?"

"Again?"

"I recall a time when you were outside her house with binoculars."

"Oh yeah, the time that *you* were there too."

"Only because you asked me to. *You* were the one who wanted to stay there all night just to see if Lori's date showed up. We nearly got busted by the neighbors. Anyway, stop trying to change the subject. Seriously, what are you doing?"

"Be quiet, I'm trying to listen."

"Fine, I'll just ask the girls what you're doing instead."

I prod a finger into his chest and whisper, "Don't you fucking dare."

"Then start talking."

"I've lost my cell," I lie. "I just came back to look for it."

"Your cell?" I nod. "You mean the one in your pocket?" he asks, pointing to it.

"There it is! No wonder I couldn't find it. Thanks, Brother." Judging by the look on his face, he's already bored of this little game. I gesture for him to follow me and don't stop until we're at the other end of the hallway. "Do you want to know the truth or the *ugly* truth?"

"Ugly. Always."

"I don't want a lecture."

"Okay," he says, looking worried.

"I had sex with Lori last night," I blurt out.

"Has she ended things with John then?"

I wince. "No." He closes his eyes and when he opens them, I see the disappointment. "Look, I know what you're probably thinking."

"What am I probably thinking?"

"That this is just me being me. Typical Buzz. That this was some drunken fuck or some kind of dick measuring contest but it was neither of those things."

"Then what was it?"

"It was how it should be all the damn time. It was us. Just us."

"But that's the thing. It's not just you two. There are three of you."

"I don't need the reminder."

He raises an eyebrow. "Are you sure about that?"

"Trust me. That smug, sparkly-toothed bastard is all I've been thinking about these past few days."

"Are you having sex with him too?"

"Fuck off."

"I had to check. Seriously though, your happiness will always mean more to me than any of Lori's boyfriends, but I don't want your happiness to be the cause of somebody else's pain. You need to do the right thing, Brother."

"I'm trying."

"Try harder."

"Yes, Boss." I follow him into the lounge and my stomach rumbles when I eye the pizza boxes.

"You could try a little harder at work too," he says, handing me a plate.

"And *you* could try a little harder to stop being such a dick."

He places a hand over his heart. "How dare you. I bought you *pizza*."

"It's a start," I reply as I open one of the boxes. I choose the slice with the most jalapeños on and I'm just about to take a bite when a cell begins to vibrate on the table next to me. I look down and see John's name flashing across the brightly lit screen. I throw the pizza back onto the plate and wipe my hand before bending down to pick it up.

"Is that Sophia's or Lori's?" Mason asks.

148

I don't answer him. Instead, I answer the call. "Lori's a little preoccupied at the minute," I drawl.

"Who is this?"

"Come on, John. You should know who it is. We've spent a lot of time together recently."

His voice turns to steel. "Where's Lori? Why have you got her cell?"

"Hmmm, which question do you want me to answer first?"

"Where's Lori?" he asks again through clenched teeth.

"She's busy." I take a bite of pizza then moan. "Mmmmm, so good. Just how I like it."

Mason appears in front of me, arms folded. "You're not trying very hard."

I wave him away and take another bite of pizza. "Who was that?" John asks.

"Mason."

"I thought Lori and Sophia were having dinner alone."

"Well you thought wrong. Plans change, John. People change too. You better get used to it."

"Put Lori on the damn phone."

"She's tied up at the moment."

"I'm not in the mood for your games."

"Bye then."

"Don't you dare hang…"

I dare. Of course I dare. I end the call then place her cell back on the table in the exact same position as it was. I fall backwards onto the couch and catch Mason staring at me. "What?" I ask, innocently.

"Did you really have to do that?"

"Yeah, I really did."

"But you're certain that this isn't a dick measuring contest…"

"Correct. But if it was, I'd win."

"I'm a little worried how you would even know that."

I shrug. "Lori didn't deny it."

"You spoke to Lori about the size of his dick? That is *so* fucked up."

"You can say that again."

"That is so…" he stops talking mid-sentence when Lori and Sophia walk into the room. He points to the pizza box, recovering quickly. "Delicious. That pizza is *so* delicious."

"The best in town," I add. "Will you two be joining us?"

Please say yes.

"Well I'm not about to turn down the best pizza in town," Lori says.

"That's my girl," I reply, not even realizing what I've said until the room fills with an awkward silence. I take a bite of pizza just as Lori's phone starts to vibrate once more. I glance down and see John's name on the screen. *Stalker.*

She walks over and scoops it up before typing out a quick text. I take a bite of pizza to hide my smug smile when she turns the power off afterwards.

"What are we watching?" Sophia asks as she sits down next to Mason.

"I thought we could try a new crime documentary."

"Boring," I reply.

He throws the remote at me. "Then you choose something."

Lori rolls her eyes when I type 'porn' into the search bar.

I laugh when it brings up some results. "I didn't actually think it would find anything.
Porn star documentaries…interesting."

"Don't pretend that you haven't already tried searching for it before today," Sophia says.

"Why would I need to when I've got the entire internet at my fingertips?"

"Been watching a lot of porn recently, Buzz?" Mason asks.

"Ah, you know. A bit of librarian porn here and there."

Lori almost chokes on her pizza.

I click onto the homepage and look at what's trending. "Huh. Beautiful Disaster. Remember when we all went to watch that at the movies? Oh wait…Mason didn't actually watch it because he was too busy being a drama queen."

"I was in the hospital having an anaphylactic shock."

"Or you were just trying to get some alone time with Sophia..."

He winks. "Well she *does* have an excellent bedside manner."

"And you know how much it turns me on when you *can't breathe*," she says sarcastically.

"Kinky," I reply.

"The Fault in Our Stars," Lori says, pointing at the screen. "Let's watch that."

"What is it?" I ask.

"A movie about two kids with cancer. It's based on the book by John Green."

"Oh wow, you've really sold it to me. We should watch it right away. Press play immediately."

She sits down next to me and takes the controller off me. "Shut up and watch it. It's awesome."

As long as she's next to me, I don't care what we watch.

CHAPTER EIGHTEEN

"Well?" she asks as soon as the credits start to roll.

"It was okay," I reply, trying to play it cool.

"Just okay?"

I shrug. "It was good."

"Good. Hmmmm."

"Jesus Christ, woman. At least give me a minute to process it all."

She leans a little closer. "Is that a tear in your eye?"

"No. Maybe. Shush."

She laughs. "It's awesome, just admit it."

"I'll admit it. It was fucking awesome. It almost made me cry three times. There. Happy now?"

She smiles smugly. "I told you."

I gesture to Mason and Sophia who are both asleep on the couch opposite us. "It's nice to see that those two enjoyed it."

"If I had a dime for every time Sophia fell asleep during a movie, I'd be a rich woman."

About a minute passes where we do nothing except stare at the two of them wrapped up in each other's arms. I want what they have so bad. I want Lori in my arms. I want to fall asleep with her at night and wake up with her every morning. I want to turn back time and stop myself from making one of the worst decisions of my life. I would love to know what Lori's thinking right now. Maybe her thoughts aren't so different to mine. Or maybe she's thinking about falling asleep in John's arms tonight. The thought kills me so I quickly say something, *anything*, just to change the subject. "You could have warned me that it was so damn emotional."

"I told you it was about cancer. I thought that was enough of a warning."

"I thought it was going to be depressing but it was actually really inspiring. It makes you stop and think about your life."

"That's why I love it so much. It's thought provoking."

"It's a good reminder that life is short," I simply say even though I want to elaborate.

I don't want to spend another second without you.

I don't want to sit back and watch you live your life with somebody else.

She nods. "The book is even better."

"You always say that."

"That's because it's always true."

"Maybe we should come up with a code word like they did," I suggest.

"A code word? Why would we need one?"

I laugh nervously. "I don't know. Just forget I said anything."

"You can't dangle the carrot in front of me and then snatch it away."

"I just thought it might be useful if we could somehow tell each other how we were feeling..."

"Without actually telling each other?"

I nod. "Exactly. There are things that I shouldn't be saying to you anymore. Things that I still want to say. Things that I'm constantly thinking."

"Like what?" she asks.

There's a long pause and I swear that I see Sophia move in the corner of my eye, but I refuse to look away from Lori. "Like I'm terrified that the longer we spend apart, the easier it will become. I know it sounds selfish but I don't want it to be easy. I don't want you to be able to live without me."

"I'm not sure I can."

"I fucking hope not."

We're silent for another moment until she takes hold of my hand and says, "But that's what I need to find out."

My heart aches but I nod. "My mom thinks that if we're truly meant to be together then we will find our way back to each other."

"Your mom's a smart lady. I love her."

"She loves you too. When she first met you, she didn't stop talking about you for a whole week afterwards. She was telling strangers in the street about how beautiful her future grandchildren were going to be. I think she probably loves you more than she loves me."

"No way. You're her little boy. She would do absolutely anything for you."

I raise an eyebrow in an attempt to lighten the mood. "Little? You know there's nothing little about me, sweetheart."

She rolls her eyes. "Her *little* boy with a *huge*…"

"Penis," I offer.

"Ego," she says.

I laugh but our smiles quickly fade. "She told me that I should give you some time to let you 'write your story'."

"I think that would be best."

"I want to be in your story so fucking bad, Lor."

"You'll always be a part of my story."

"But I don't just want to be a part of it. I want to be your happy ever after. It feels like I'm trying so hard to be the hero that I've somehow ended up being the villain."

"If you're a villain then what does that make me?"

The doorbell rings causing Mason to jump up off the couch. "Where am I?" Sophia simply opens her eyes and looks straight at us. I'm pretty sure that she was already awake. Her eyes turn sad when she notices our linked hands. My heart aches when Lori pulls away, her cheeks reddening.

"How long was I asleep for?" Mason asks, looking around the room.

"Did you see the part where they went into space?" I ask.

"Into space?"

"Ignore him," Sophia says as she stands up. "We fell asleep about twenty minutes ago. I'll get the door."

"No, it's late. Let me get it."

She nods and watches him leave the room before turning her attention to us. "Are you both okay?"

"Fine," Lori answers.

"And I'm fine if Lori's fine," I say.

"I need to call an Uber," she says, stretching her legs.

"You can stay over if you want?" Sophia asks.

"Can I stay over too?" I ask with a grin. "You've got enough bedrooms."

"Not a chance," she replies.

Lori pulls her cell out of her pocket just as John walks into the room. *What the fuck is he doing here?* His eyes widen when he spots us sitting next to each other on the couch. I hear Lori sigh as he looks around at all the candles and blankets. "Well this looks cozy."

It was until you got here, dickhead.

"Nice evening?" he asks nobody in particular.

"Delightful," I reply. "Intimate." I'm pretty sure everybody except for John rolls their eyes.

"What are you doing here?" Lori asks as she stands up. My eyes automatically shoot to her ass and when I manage to tear them away, John is looking at me like he wants to kill me. I wink at him just to wind him up even more. "I was worried," he says through clenched teeth. "You weren't answering your cell."

"Sorry. It ran out of battery," she lies. I don't even try to hide my smirk. "I told you I was getting an Uber home."

155

"And that's why I was worried." *No. You were worried that she was fucking me.* He looks straight at me as he says, "I don't trust them."

I guess he's not talking about Uber's anymore. "That's a pretty bold statement to make when you don't even know them," I reply.

"I've heard enough about them. They have a bad reputation. I don't want my girlfriend alone with them, especially at night."

I don't know why we're even bothering with discreet insults and passive aggressive bullshit. It's blatantly obvious what we're talking about. "People change, remember?" I ask him, referring to our earlier phone conversation.

"We should probably go," Lori says.

"Yeah, let's go home," he says, throwing a smug smile in my direction. "It's been a long day. I can't wait to get into bed."

Prick.

"Is there room for one more?" I ask.

"Excuse me?" John asks, blinking so fast he looks like he's having an epileptic fit.

"In your car. Can I catch a ride home?"

Lori shoots me a pointed look as I stand up, not bothering to wait for his reply. "Thanks for the awesome evening, guys," I say to Mason and Sophia. "Good food and even better company. It was just like the good old days. We should do it more often."

"I can give you a ride," Mason says, purposely trying to diffuse another awkward situation.

"You've had too much to drink," I reply, even though he's only had one beer. "John doesn't mind, do you, John?"

"Of course not," he replies with a fake smile. "Anything to help out one of Lori's *friends*."

"Friends with benefits," I correct him.

Lori spins around, wide eyed.

"What did you just say?" John says, doing the weird blinking thing again.

"I'm getting a free ride home." I shrug. "That's what I call friends with benefits."

Lori glares at me as she walks over to Sophia and Mason and kisses them both on the cheek. "I'll call you tomorrow."

I follow her and nudge Mason with my shoulder. "Thanks for feeding me, Brother."

"And for beating you at pool?"

"Nah, I let you win."

"Of course you did." He leans in closer and lowers his voice as he says, "Remember to try harder. Try real hard."

"Believe me, I'm trying."

I give Sophia a quick hug. "Sweet dreams, Soph."

"Play nice," she whispers.

"Always," I reply.

"Night, guys," John says. "You should come over to my house one night next week. I'll cook you dinner. It's always nice to mix with other *couples*."

I laugh at how much I want to punch him in the face right now. They all say goodnight as I keep my focus on Lori, reminding myself why I'm putting myself through this.

As soon as their front door closes, the tension in the air becomes unbearable. Three is most definitely a crowd. I walk slightly ahead of them so I don't have to watch them hold hands and head straight over to his stupid silver car. I lean against it, arms crossed as I wait for them to catch me up.

John frowns. "How do you know this is my car?"

Oh, shit. "I saw it when I dropped by your office yesterday," I say as casually as I can.

"I didn't drive to work yesterday," he replies flatly. "I cycled."

"Of course you did." I don't remember the last time I rode a bike. My Harley, sure, but not a bicycle. "Hmmmm, I must have seen it at the dinner party the other night."

"Yeah, you drove us that night," Lori adds but he doesn't look convinced.

"Plus," I say, pointing to his registration plate. "It doesn't take a genius to figure out that this is your car. It quite clearly says Dr *Clown*." If looks could kill, I'd be ten feet under by now.

"Speaking of which," he says. "You'll be receiving an invoice for a new door plaque seeing as though you defaced my last one."

"That's fine. Do I get to choose what name goes on it?" I chuckle when Lori raises her eyebrow at me.

"No." He unlocks the car and makes his way around to the driver's side.

I quickly cover her hand with mine just as she's about to open the passenger side door. "Twenty eight," I whisper.

She frowns. "What?"

"Our code word. Well, I guess it's more of a code number..."

"Why twenty eight? What does it mean?"

"It's a reminder of how much..."

"Is there a problem?" John asks from the other side of the car.

Aside from the fact that you exist? I refuse to move my hand as I say, "We were just deciding who gets to ride shotgun."

"And of course I win," she adds as she opens the door, forcing me to let go of her hand.

I give a low whistle as I climb into the back and slide across the seats. "Leather. Nice. The first car I ever owned had leather seats. Fun but sticky."

He looks at me in his rear-view mirror. "Excuse me?"

158

"Sweaty skin on leather can be a pain in the ass…well, *on* the ass."

"I wouldn't know."

"You mean you haven't christened this thing?"

"Cars are for driving," is all he says.

Boring bastard. "Try telling that to seventeen-year-old me. Asking a girl if she wanted a ride meant an entirely different thing." My eyes find Lori's in the passenger side mirror and even though she rolls her eyes, I can tell that she's blushing. We drive for a few seconds in silence. "So how much did the personalized plate cost?" I ask.

"I don't know. It was a gift."

"From who?"

"A friend."

"I knew Mason was a shitty friend for only buying me socks at Christmas."

"Which friend?" Lori asks.

"Oh, you don't know them."

Which is actually code for *let's stop talking about this*. So naturally, I do the opposite. "What's their name?"

He pauses before answering. "Tanya."

I see. "That's a nice name," I say, stirring the pot. "She sounds like a great *friend*."

"Why haven't I heard about her?" Lori asks.

"I don't see her that much anymore, babe."

"That much," I point out.

"What?" he asks, sounding annoyed.

"You don't see her *that much*. So how often *do* you see her?"

"Once every few weeks. We're both busy. She's a doctor too."

"A doctor or a dentist?" *I can't help it.*

Lori looks over her shoulder but doesn't scold me. Instead she asks, "How do you know her?"

"From college."

"Did you two date?" she asks.

Another pause.

Bad move.

"No," he answers.

"You had to think about that one," I say with a chuckle.

"I'm trying to concentrate on driving," he lies.

"Have you ever slept with her?" I push.

"That's none of your business."

"Answer the question," Lori says.

He glances at me before placing a hand on her knee. "Can we talk about this later, babe?"

"No. I'd rather talk about it now."

He sighs. "We messed around a few times but it was nothing serious. It was years ago."

"Then why would she buy you a personalized registration plate?" She asks before I get the chance to.

"Because we used to be good friends. She bought it me as a gift when I officially passed all of my exams and became a doctor."

"Dentist," I correct him. They both ignore me and act as though I'm not even in the car which stings a little.

"I just don't get why it's the first time I'm hearing about her if she used to be a big part of your life."

"You just said it yourself. She *used* to be a big part of my life. Not anymore. I've only seen her a handful of times since we started dating."

"And yet you haven't mentioned her once."

"I'm pretty sure you haven't mentioned every single one of your friends to me."

"I doubt any of her *friends* have bought her a gift worth thousands of dollars. *Tens* of thousands."

"This has got nothing to do with you," John spits.

"Apparently it's got nothing to do with Lori either," I fire back.

"That's enough," Lori says. "I don't want to talk about it anymore."

So we don't.

We sit in silence for the rest of the journey except for when I grunt directions. I look at Lori in the passenger side mirror and it hurts me that *she* looks hurt. I don't want her to care that he has female friends who buy him expensive gifts. I want her to care about me. *Only me.*

"Which house?" he asks as we pull onto my street.

"Number three one six," I tell him. "Half way down on the left."

He slows to a stop and I wonder if Lori is thinking about coming here last night. "What are you doing?" John asks as she opens the door.

"I need to stretch my legs," she tells him before slamming the door shut.

He says something else but I'm already half way out of the car and following her towards the house. "Hey," I say as I fall into step beside her. "Are you okay?"

"Yeah," she lies. "Why wouldn't I be?"

"The Tanya thing."

She shrugs. "I guess I'm not in a position to lecture him about other women after what we did, am I?"

"Don't be like that."

"Like what? It's true."

"No, it's not. Two wrongs don't make a right. If he fucks with you, I swear I'll ruin more than just his door plaque."

"Oh shut up with the alpha stuff, Buzz."

"I'm being serious. I'll deface his face."

"Well you can save your breath because he's not going to *fuck with me.* I trust him."

We stop walking when we reach my front door. "You sure about that?"

"I'm sure."

I look over at his car. "You sounded a little jealous back there."

"I know and that's why I'm pissed off. I'm pissed at myself for doubting him. I'm pissed that because of what happened yesterday, my brain instantly jumped to conclusions. Stupid conclusions. And I'm also pissed at you for being such a shit stirrer."

"Me, a shit stirrer?" I chuckle then gesture to the door. "Want to come inside?"

"No, Buzz."

"So you just wanted to walk me to my door? How romantic of you."

"Don't flatter yourself. I just needed some air."

"Well feel free to breathe the air directly outside my front door whenever you want." She rolls her eyes. "And if it's cold air, I'll be in here waiting to warm you up. And if it's hot air, we can jump in the shower to cool off."

She shakes her head but laughs. "I should get back."

"Do I get a kiss goodnight?"

She raises her eyebrow. "Stop it."

"What?" I ask, feigning innocence. "Mason got one."

"Goodnight, Buzz," she repeats as she walks away. After a few steps, she turns back around. "I almost forgot...what does twenty eight mean?"

I smile but my heart clenches. "To infinity."

She looks confused. "I don't understand."

"Two and eight. Swap out the *number* two with the *word* to and then the eight is an infinity sign. To infinity."

"Oh. I've never looked at it like that before."

"See." I wink. "Nobody will crack our code."

"So wait...when I see the number twenty eight, I'm supposed to think about what? You calling it out during sex?"

I laugh. "If that's what you want to think about then sure, go ahead." I take a couple of steps forward, closing the gap between us. I know that I shouldn't touch her when John is no doubt watching us but I can't help it. I reach out and tuck a loose strand of hair behind her ear. "But maybe it can also be a little reminder of how I feel

162

about you. If I ever did anything right in my life, it was opening my heart to you. The second I met you, I knew you were the kind of girl that I could be with forever, to infinity and beyond." I have to stop myself from pulling her into my arms and begging her to give us another shot. "Nothing has changed for me, Lor."

She's about to reply just as John shouts, "You coming, babe?"

I glance over and see him standing next to his car. He looks annoyed but mostly terrified which isn't all that different to how I'm feeling right now. Annoyed at the thought of losing Lori to him…terrified that it might have already happened.

Something flashes in her eyes and for a split second, I convince myself that she's about to tell him no but then the moment passes and I'm brought back down to earth with a thud as she sighs and says, "Goodnight, Buzz."

"Goodnight, Lor," I reply, trying not to sound too defeated.

I watch her walk back to the car.
Back to him.

CHAPTER NINETEEN

I don't talk to her for a whole year.

It's actually only two weeks but it might as well be a year.

It *feels* like a year.

The days are long and the nights are even longer. I can't sleep for more than a few hours and I've been eating out most evenings as I can't even bear to be in my own kitchen after what happened in there the other week.

I've gone a lot longer without talking to her, but this time feels different. *It feels wrong.* I've wanted to call her. Hell, I *have* called her - several times. But I always cancelled the call before it even had the chance to ring.

On day fifteen, she puts me out of my misery. I'm walking into work when her name flashes across my cell. I take a deep breath before greeting her with, "Twenty eight." I can't hold it in any longer.

"Excuse me?" John replies.

John.

"What's up?" I ask. "Is Lori okay?"

He laughs. "Of course Lori's okay. I wouldn't be calling *you* if she wasn't."

"Then why *are* you calling me?"

A pause and then, "I'm extending an olive branch."

I stop walking. "Why?"

"Because as much as I dislike you, my girlfriend can see something in you which I clearly can't."

I have to stop myself from asking him if he's referring to my dick. "So you want to braid my hair?"

"Not quite. I'm inviting you to dinner."

"When?"

"This Thursday. Seven o'clock."

"Perfect. My favorite day of the week."

"Mason can give you my address. He's coming too."

"Do I need to dress up for you?" I ask sarcastically.

"I'd prefer it if you wore clothes, yes."

"Oh, so you *can* be funny."

"I can be a lot of things."

My heart sinks when I hear Lori's voice somewhere in the background. "You ready to go?" she asks, and I desperately wish that I was the one answering her.

"I have to go. See you on Thursday," John says before quickly hanging up.

I blink and then look around, unsure what to do next. A few seconds later, I realize that I still have my cell pressed up against my ear. When I finally slip it back into my pocket, I wonder how she managed to sound so normal when I feel so...empty.

Roll on Thursday because I have every intention of finding out.

"You look miserable," Mason says as I walk into his office later that day carrying a huge stack of papers.

I dump them onto his desk. "That's because I am."

"What's happened?"

"Lori happened," I reply as I walk over to the huge floor-to-ceiling windows lining the back wall of his office. "Nothing new." I peer out at the street some fifty floors below and wonder how I've ended up here. How out of billions of people in the world, I'm in love with a woman I can't have.

Mason appears next to me and places a hand on my shoulder. "Everything will be okay, Brother. I know it might not feel like it right now, but everything happens for a reason."

"My mom has already given me the fate speech but thanks."

We're quiet for a moment before he asks, "Have you spoken to her? To Lori, I mean."

I spin around to face him. "No. Have you?"

"Yeah, she came by the house last night."

"How is she?"

"It's hard to tell. She *says* she's doing okay but she didn't seem her usual self." He nudges my shoulder playfully. "She wasn't staring out of any windows though. I remember a time not too long ago when you mocked me for staring out of a window. What was it that you said? Ah yeah, you said that I was acting like I was in a romcom. Something about needing tissues and Ben and Jerry's. Do you remember that?"

"Fuck you."

"I have a fiancée for that."

"Smug bastard," I mutter as I walk over to the leather couch and fall down onto it. I run a hand through my hair. "Be honest with me now. Do you think she's happy with him?"

"I honestly don't know. She seems different these days. I sometimes get little glimpses of the old Lori. The one we first met. You know, before..." he trails off.

"Before I broke her heart?" I say, finishing his sentence for him.

He shrugs. "She might be happy with him but I've seen her happier."

"John called me this morning."

He narrows his eyes. "Why?"

"He's invited me to dinner at his house on Thursday."

"Huh, that's weird."

"Yeah, I think he's up to something but I haven't figured out what yet."

"We've been invited too. He told us it was a game night."

"Cool. Lori can watch me beat his ass."

"He told me it was a game night for *couples*."

"Well it looks like I'm going to be on a team by myself." I chuckle. "He seems to have a thing for couples' nights, doesn't he? Maybe he's a swinger."

"If he is then he better not look in Sophia's direction."

"Hey, it could be fun. I'd happily fuck his girlfriend for him."

He sighs. "Buzz…"

"What? I'm joking."

"Are you though?"

"Well I'd fuck her every day for the rest of my life if I could but yeah, I said it in jest."

He shakes his head. "Just please don't say anything *in jest* on Thursday."

"I can't make any promises."

"This is a terrible idea."

"Chill out. It's going to be fine."

Famous last words.

CHAPTER TWENTY

I'm scrolling through the black hole otherwise known as Instagram that evening when my cell starts to vibrate in my hand. *Twice in one day*, I think to myself as Lori's name flashes across the screen.

"Have you changed your mind about braiding my hair?" I say in greeting, convinced that it'll be John again. He's probably about to un-invite me to his swingers night. "Hello?" I say when nobody replies.

More silence.

"Lor? Is that you?"

A sigh and then, "Yes."

My stomach flips at the sound of her voice and before I can even stop myself, I blurt out, "I miss you."

"Buzz," she warns.

"I'm sorry but it's true. I miss you so damn much. Do you know how many times I've called you before hanging up? Take a guess."

"I don't know."

"I stopped at twenty eight. Twenty eight, Lor. It seemed fitting. Please tell me that I'm not crazy. Please tell me that you think of me too and that I'm not alone in this."

Another pause and then, "You're not alone."

Thank fuck for that. I stand up and begin to pace up and down. I seem to do it a lot these days. "So how much longer are we going to do this for?"

"Do what?"

"Pretend that we're okay. Ignore our feelings."

"You're not exactly ignoring your feelings, Buzz."

"I'd be at your house right now if I wasn't ignoring my feelings. I'm guessing John told you that he called me earlier?"

"No, he didn't. I saw your name at the top of my caller list and asked him about it. He was the only person who was near my phone today." She takes a deep breath. "Do you know how long the call lasted for?"

"It wasn't long. He didn't say much."

"It was twenty eight seconds. When I saw the number next to your name, I thought it was a sign."

"A huge sign," I add. "A huge, flashing, *neon* sign."

"Please don't come on Thursday," she whispers.

My heart sinks. "Why not?"

"Because even though I stand by everything I said last week, I'm not sure I'll want you to leave."

"Then I won't. I'll stay for as long as you want me to. I'll stay forever, Lor."

"Don't come because you'll say things like that and I'm a weak woman around you."

"Is that supposed to deter me from coming because it's making me want to see you even more."

"I need more time, Buzz."

"It's only Monday; you have three more days."

"I'm trying to be serious here."

"Me too. I've cut contact with you for two weeks. I'm trying to respect you but at the same time, I also need to respect myself. Let me come on Thursday. I'll be on my best behavior, I promise."

"That's what I'm worried about."

I laugh. "Aww come on, what's the worst that could happen?"

"Hmmm, I can think of a few things."

"Oh, really? Like what?"

"I'm not about to give you any ideas."

"Why not?"

"I'm sure you can use your imagination."

"You're right, I can." My voice turns deeper. "Do you want to know what I'm imagining right now?"

"Goodnight, Buzz."

I chuckle. "I'm guessing phone sex is out of the question then?"

She hangs up and for the first time in fifteen days, I have a genuine smile on my face.

CHAPTER TWENTY ONE

"Let the games begin!" I announce as I walk through the door to John's house on Thursday.

At least, I *think* it's John's house. When nobody responds, I start to worry that I've just let myself into one of his neighbor's houses instead. "Hello?" I shout.

A door to my left opens and Sophia pokes her head out. "Oh, hey, we didn't hear the…what the *hell* are you wearing?" She bursts out laughing.

"My game night outfit, obviously." I adjust my visor and look down at my T-shirt which has a picture of a jack and a king from a deck of cards with the word 'off' underneath them. "Jacking off…really, Buzz?"

"Yes, really. You're just jealous." I eye her light blue jumpsuit. "What are *you* wearing?"

"Normal person clothes."

"Just because we're at a dentist's house, it doesn't mean you have to dress like one. You look like you're wearing scrubs."

She raises an eyebrow. "Is that the best you've got?"

"Until I think of a better insult then yes."

Mason appears behind her and shakes his head. "Why? Just…why?"

"Why what? Why am I so awesome? Why does Sophia wish you were more like me? I don't know, you'll have to ask her yourself."

Sophia rolls her eyes and then glances over my shoulder. I turn around and grin when I see Lori walking towards us. She's wearing a denim skirt and a T-shirt which says, 'I don't even fold my laundry' with a deck of playing cards underneath.

"Oh god. Not you as well," Sophia says. "Why didn't we get the memo to wear lame T-shirts?"

I tap the side of my head. "Because the memo only exists up here. You're just going to have to accept that you'll never be as cool as us." I turn to Lori and nod to her shirt, trying my hardest not to stare at her tits. "Fighting talk, huh?"

She shrugs nonchalantly. "You know me."

I grin. "I do know you. I know you *very* well."

"This is going to be a long night," she says with a sigh.

My eyes roam her perfect curves. "Oh, I hope so."

"I'm taking no shit tonight, Buzz."

My dick twitches. "I love it when you're bossy."

"I mean it."

"So do I."

We all stand in silence for a few seconds and I wish more than anything that I could turn back time to when it was just the four of us. To a time when we weren't standing in her goddamn *boyfriend's* house. I look around. "Nice place he's got. It's very…beige." Beige carpets, beige walls, beige furniture. It makes sense. A boring house for a boring guy. "Where is he, anyway?"

"He's gone to pick up some friends."

"You mean he actually has some friends?" I wink at her when she scowls. "Hey, do you want to fit in a quickie before he gets back?" Her eyes widen and she's about to protest when I add, "A quick game of UNO."

"Is that what you're calling it these days?"

"I have no idea what you're talking about, Lori."

"Of course you don't. Been getting a lot of practice in recently, have you? Been playing a lot of UNO?"

"Just the once, actually. I had an epic game of it a few weeks ago. I can't wait for the rematch."

She blushes and I have to bite the inside of my mouth to stop from laughing. "I'm going to get the snacks." She holds a hand up to me when I go to follow her. "Watch him," she instructs Sophia.

"I'll try my best," she replies, pulling me into his beige lounge with his beige walls and beige sofa. "Quit

172

winding her up," she tells me as she sits down, adjusting the beige cushion behind her.

"I'm not," I reply, feigning innocence.

"Why does it always feel like you and Lori are talking in code?" Mason asks.

Because we usually are. "No comment," I reply as I walk over to the fireplace and look up at all the frames hanging above it. Normal people have family photos, but John has dentistry certificates, all *eight* of them. "What a loser."

"Buzz," Sophia warns. "You can't talk like that tonight. You're in his house, remember?"

"How could I ever forget? All the *beige*."

"Where do you think you're going?" Sophia asks as I walk over to the door.

I wink at her. "I'm in the mood for a snack."

"Buzz, no."

Mason takes hold of her hand as she's about to stand up. "Let him do what he needs to do."

"But…"

"Before John gets back," he adds, which seems to do the trick.

She sighs. "I don't want to clean up your mess in the morning."

"There won't be any mess," I reply as I leave the room.

I head in the direction of the kitchen but pause when I see her. I watch as she opens several different cupboards, obviously looking for something. "Why don't you know where to look?"
She jumps and holds a hand over her chest. "You scared me."

"I'm sorry."

She opens another cupboard and pulls out a big plastic bowl. "Got it."

"Why didn't you know where to find it?"
"I don't come here all that much."

173

"Why not?"

She shrugs. "I prefer my own place."

I chuckle. "It's all the beige, isn't it?"

She rolls her eyes but I can tell that she wants to laugh. "Go and wait with Sophia and Mason. I don't need any help."

"You don't belong here," I reply, all joking aside.

"Where? In this kitchen?"

"In this house," I clarify even though she knew exactly what I meant.

"Well neither do you," she replies as she opens a bag of popcorn and starts to empty it into the bowl. "You shouldn't have come here."

"You mean you didn't want to see me?"

She shakes the bag, checking that there's no more popcorn left. "Let's just get tonight over with, okay?"

"You didn't answer my question."

"And I'm not going to. Tonight isn't the time for your questions."

"So when is?"

She sighs. "I don't know, Buzz. I mean, does it really matter if I want to see you or not?"

"Of course it matters. I want to be near you all the damn time, even if that means being here, in *his* house. I'll take it any day over not seeing you."

"This is difficult for me too, you know," she says, taking a step closer to me. "Seeing you here...it feels wrong. It's messing with my head. It's jumbling everything up."

"What do you mean?"

"You and John are so different. You're worlds apart. When I'm with you and when I'm with him...it's like I'm living two separate lives. It feels like I'm part of two different *worlds*. And tonight those two worlds have collided and I'm struggling to process it all."

I take another step forward, closing the gap between us. "Go on..."

She shakes her head. "When you're in the room, it's hard to ignore you. You're so *alpha*."

I try not to grin. "Then don't ignore me."

"I need to but it's so hard. I feel like I'm at an AA meeting and you're the cold bottle of beer, urging me to take a drink."

"So what you're trying to say is that you want a taste of me? You want to drink me?"

She rolls her eyes. "I'm saying that you're a walking temptation."

"So what does that make John? Your sponsor?"

As if I've somehow magically summoned him, the front door opens and I hear his annoying nasally voice float down the hallway.

Lori sighs as she takes a step backwards. "Please don't start any trouble."

"Not all addictions are bad, you know," I tell her, gently pulling her back to me. "Sometimes they're just what a person needs. They can satisfy you in ways other things can't. In ways other *people* can't."

She shakes free of my grasp and holds the bowl of popcorn with two hands. "That's exactly what I'm afraid of."

I try to process her words as I watch her leave the room. I run a hand through my hair and take a deep breath before following her out. I only take a few steps before stopping at the sight of John and his friends, or rather, *friend*...who also happens to be his assistant.

John looks straight past Lori and instead grins at me. "Buzz, I'm glad you could make it." He gestures to the pretty blonde standing next to him. I can't remember her name. Hailey, I think. "You already know Hannah, don't you?" *Close enough.* He winks at me suggestively and now I know the real reason why he invited here tonight. He's trying to pimp Hannah out while also making it look like something has already happened between us. Judging by the look on Lori's face, his plan is working.

175

"It's great to see you again," Hannah says, looking me up and down. I wonder if she's in on the plan or if she genuinely wants to fuck me. It's probably the latter.

"How do you two know each other?" Lori asks, acting so laid back that she sounds bored. "UNO, perhaps?"

I raise an eyebrow at her and she raises one right back. I can't believe she's getting jealous right now when I'm the one standing in her boyfriend's house. Even so, it feels pretty damn good to know that she cares. I'm about to answer when Hannah excitedly says, "Oooh, I love UNO!" I chuckle when I see the look on Lori's face. "Are we playing it tonight?" she asks.

"I don't know," Lori replies. "*Will* you be playing it tonight, Buzz?"

"I'd love to play UNO with you tonight, Lori. If it were up to me, we'd play it all night long."

"Yay!" Hannah says, clapping her hands. "Count me in!"

"Oh, even better," I joke, which Lori doesn't appreciate.

"Actually, I think we should skip UNO tonight," Mason says, appearing next to me. "I've just cracked the code," he whispers in my ear.

Hannah pouts and this time last year, I would be obsessing over those full, cherry colored lips. Obsessing over what she could do with them…and where she could put them. And I would make it my mission to find out. But now it's such a fleeting thought and my only mission is to save Lori from a beige life when she deserves technicolor. I know that I could give her all the colors of the rainbow but for that to happen, I have to put up with a giant fucking downpour first. I knew John was a drip as soon as I saw him.

"Aww, maybe another night then?" Hannah asks, breaking me free from my thoughts.

"Oh, I'm sure Buzz would be happy to oblige you," Lori tells her, flashing a fake smile before staking off into the lounge.

I zoom in on her ass until it's blocked by John, gesturing for us to follow him. "Come and sit down, make yourselves comfortable. I want you to feel like this is your home as well as *ours*."

He smirks at me and I fall right into his trap. "I didn't know you were living together."

"We're not," Lori replies.

"Not yet," John adds, wrapping his arm around her and pulling her close to him. "But we might as well be. You spend so much time here."

Lying bastard. "Would you say that you know your way around each other's kitchens?" I ask. "You know where everything is kept?"

He looks at me like I'm crazy. "Yes, Buzz. I'm well acquainted with her kitchen. I'm well acquainted with her bedroom too."

Sophia chokes on a piece of popcorn and it's enough of a distraction to stop me from blurting out '*me too*'.

"TMI, boss," Hannah says, giggling, as Sophia reassures Mason that she's okay.

"I didn't mean it like that," John says with a chuckle. "I'm especially excited about Lori's bedroom because she's finally given me my very own drawer."

My heart aches. Who would have thought the mention of a drawer could hurt this fucking much?

"I've had a toothbrush over there for quite some time now," he continues. "But this is definitely a step up."

My eyes find Lori's and it's like looking in a mirror.

I see *regret*.

I have to stop myself from asking her what, or who, she regrets. Him or me?

Fuck, I hate feeling like this. Like I'm a prisoner trapped inside my own body with all these emotions. No wonder I've stayed away from relationships for so long. From *love* for so long. I glance at John and he's completely oblivious to what's going on around him. He's too busy grinning at me, waiting for my reaction. Too busy with his dick measuring contest. All it would take is one look at Lori to realize that something's not right. Maybe he doesn't care. Maybe he would rather have a piece of her heart than none at all. I can't blame him. After all, isn't that what I'm doing?

"What about you, Buzz?" John asks. "Given out any toothbrushes lately?" Lori's head snaps up. Apparently her feet aren't all that interesting anymore.

I pause, letting her sweat a little while longer. "Nah, I don't do sleepovers."

Unless it's with your girlfriend.

"You'll always have a toothbrush at my house, buddy," Mason says.

My best friend is better than yours. I blow him a kiss. "Thanks, Brother. Can I have my own drawer too?"

"Of course."

"What about a fancy-ass walk-in wardrobe?"

"What's mine is yours."

I wink at Sophia. "Did you hear that, Soph?" She sighs but carries on eating the popcorn. I turn back to Mason. "Well she didn't say no."

"Too far, Bro."

Hannah giggles but John is looking at us like we're a different species. I can't imagine the guys at dentistry school have much banter. Speaking of which..."Is it just the six of us tonight?"

"Yes. Nice and *intimate.*"

My fist would like to get intimate with his face. "Where are the rest of your friends?"

"They're busy."

I chuckle. "Having fun with their other friends?"

"A lot of my friends are doctors so they work evenings."

A lot of his friends are also imaginary. "Real doctors?" I ask. "Or dentists like you?"

"Yes, Buzz. *Real* doctors."

"Jeez, I wonder how many certificates *they* have."

He ignores me and turns to Hannah. "Sit with Buzz. You'll look after Han tonight, won't you, Buzz?"

Lori raises an eyebrow at me so I smile sweetly at her. "Of course I will."

See how she likes it.

"Excellent," John replies, clapping his hands together. "So, what are we all drinking?"

"Whatever you've got," I reply, when what I really mean is *whatever will get me drunk the quickest.*

"I have a nice 2015 Sauvignon Blanc."

Of course he does. "I'll take a nice 2019 beer, if you've got one."

"A beer? You're missing out, Buzz," he says, glancing at Lori before giving me a pointed look. "You're *seriously* missing out." I'm not stupid, I know what he's doing and two can play that fucking game. Apparently Lori isn't the only one who likes to talk to me in code. "I can assure you that it tastes delicious," he adds. "Spicy. Sensual. *Full bodied.*"

"I know exactly how good it tastes," I spit back. "I can drink the wine whenever I want to, John." I take a couple of steps backwards and sit down, grinning. "I'm just taking a little break right now."

"It won't be there for you when you decide you want it again. It's mine and I'll sure as hell enjoy drinking it tonight." I have no idea how I have so much self-control. "You had your chance but you didn't want it," he continues.

"I've always wanted it."

"No. You chose the beer. You like the *easier* options. The *cheaper* ones."

179

"You don't know me. Don't tell me what I like."

"You don't know how to fully appreciate wine, Buzz. Special wines need to be respected and well looked after."

Fuck this.

I turn to face Lori. "What do you think, Lori? What do *you* want?" She looks pissed off so naturally, I continue. "Do you want the wine, or do you want a taste of the *nice, cold beer*?" I ask, referring to our earlier conversation in the kitchen.

She smiles but it's completely unnerving. "Actually, none of them appeal to me right now." I laugh. Of course she's playing along. "I think I'll stick to water for the foreseeable future."

"Well if you change your mind, let me know."

"My house, my drinks," John replies. "I can fulfil her needs, whatever they are."

"Are you sure about that?" I challenge, standing up.

"Yes," he replies, and we stare at each other until Lori sighs. "I'll get the drinks." John goes to respond but she cuts him off. "*I'll* get them. Mason, what are you drinking?"

He looks so awkward, I actually feel a little bit sorry for him. "Oh, um…well after that…I don't…I guess I'll take a beer. I think. Do you even have beer?"

"Yes," is all she replies. "Hannah?"

She giggles. "I'll take the wine if nobody else is having it."

"How considerate of you," Lori replies sarcastically before walking out of the room.

John goes to follow her but I place a hand on his shoulder, pressing down firmly. "Hey, you stay here. You're the host, remember? Stay with your guests. I can help Lori *fulfil her needs*." Sophia sighs as I leave the room.

When I walk into the kitchen, Lori is waiting for me, hands on her hips, scowl on her face. It's so fucking hot. "Do you think it's a coincidence that we keep seeing each other on a Thursday?"

"Will you ever shut up about Throwback Thursday?"

"Probably not."

She shakes her head. "I think you should leave."

"Why? I like being here with you. I even like this kitchen because you're in it. I think I've spent more time in here than I have my own kitchen. I can't even remember the last time I was in there." I pretend to look like I'm deep in thought. "Oh wait…yes I do." She narrows her eyes, knowing exactly what's coming. "We were in there two weeks ago, weren't we?"

"You need to leave."

I take a step closer to her. "And *you* need to have a beer."

"I don't want the beer."

I smirk. "You always *want* the beer, Lori. You just feel pressured into drinking the pompous wine."

"Pressured by who?"

"Yourself. Society."

"Is that right?"

"Yep."

"Has your arrogant ass ever stopped to think that maybe the *pompous wine* tastes nice?"

"It tastes shit and we both know it." I shake my head, becoming impatient. You're just doing that thing."

She throws her hands up. "What thing?"

"That thing where you're supposed to eat or drink something you don't like twelve times before you're eventually supposed to like it. You're trying to alter your taste buds."

She narrows her eyes. "For starters, I've always liked Joh…" she stops herself before continuing. "I've always liked *the wine* to begin with and secondly, I've drank it, or eaten it, whatever shitty analogy you want to use, way more than twelve times now."

181

Ouch. I don't let her see how much her words affect me. "Yet you're still not satisfied, are you? You've still got to eat your fill in other people's kitchens."

"You're such a dick."

"The truth hurts, doesn't it?"

"What *hurts* is the fact that you broke up with me then came running back when I met somebody else."

"You know what also hurts? The fact that you've met somebody else but *keep* running back to me."

"Then I won't. I'll stop."

"I don't want you to stop. I want you to come back to me for good. There's a huge difference."

She sighs. "We've been through this."

"Well I want to go through it again."

"Like I told you earlier - now isn't the time. Why don't you just leave and take Hannah with you?"

"What's Hannah got to do with any of this?"

She raises her eyebrow. "I don't know. You tell me."

"No, *you* tell *me*. Spit it out."

"When did you fuck her?"

"Who says that I've fucked her?"

"I do. She's a female with a pulse."

"Being a bitch doesn't suit you, Lor."

"It's obvious you've had sex by the way she keeps looking at you."

"All women look at me like that."

"Just answer the damn question."

I smirk. "Tonight isn't the time for questions, remember? You said so yourself."

I can see the rage swirling in her eyes and I'm glad she doesn't know where the knives are kept. "Do you get a medal or something for fucking every woman in San Francisco?"

"I don't know. I sure hope so."

"Just tell me this…was it before or after I *ate my fill* in your kitchen?"

182

"Oh, remind me, was that before or after you gave John his own drawer?"

"I didn't give him one, he asked for one."

"That's the same thing."

"No it isn't."

"In that case, please can I have a drawer in your bedroom? Can I have my own side of the bed too? Actually, why don't you just go ahead and give me a spare key?"

"I'm guessing the fact that you're avoiding my question is answer enough."

"I haven't fucked her, Lori."

"Hmmmm."

"I wouldn't lie to you."

"Do you *plan* on fucking her?"

"Do you plan on fucking John?"

"That's different."

I laugh. "I thought it might be."

"I'm in a relationship with him."

"So that makes it all okay."

"No, what I'm trying to say…"

"Is everything okay in here?" A voice asks from the doorway. I turn around to see John holding onto the doorframe. He looks too calm to have heard much but too disappointed to have heard nothing. "What's the hold up?"

"Oh, um, I couldn't find the bottle opener," Lori lies.

He walks over to us slowly and grabs the bottle opener straight off the counter. "It's right here."

"Well no wonder we couldn't find it. I was looking in all of the drawers."

John looks at the both of us and I know that he knows. *He* knows that *I* know that *he* knows. I wait for him to say something, to question us about it, to hit me, but he doesn't. He simply opens the fridge and pulls several beers out before handing them to me. "Can you take these into the other room?"

I don't want to leave her but she gives me a little nod. "Of course," I reply. "Give me a shout if you need anything else."

"Nah, we're good," John replies.

Are they? I walk away and for a split second, I consider bailing. I could take the beers and run but I meant what I said. I'd rather be with her in his house than not be with her at all. And for right now, I'd rather own a piece of her heart than nothing at all.

CHAPTER TWENTY TWO

The next hour consists of snide digs, stolen glances and the most awkward game that was ever invented. I've always loved Cards Against Humanity and tonight was no different. One of my highlights was when John picked the question card 'What ended my last relationship?' and I answered with, 'A micropenis'. I wasn't surprised when he chose 'Crippling debt' as the winner. *Boring bastard.* Similarly, Lori didn't find it funny when she read out 'A romantic candlelit dinner would be incomplete without...' and my answer was 'Pulling out'.

"I'm pretty sure that game was invented for you," Hannah says when the game is over.

"Oh, didn't you know?" I reply. "My job is to write the answers."

Mason chuckles. "Wait. I'm your boss so that means I invented the whole game. I'm not sure how I feel about that."

"The quiet ones are always the worst."

"Wow," Hannah says, wide eyed. "That's so cool."

Lori rolls her eyes. "He's lying to you."

Hannah snorts. "Oh! Duh! I'm so freaking gullible sometimes."

"Nah, it's just that Buzz is such a good liar. He's very convincing when he feeds people his lines. Don't blame yourself." She downs the rest of her water then gestures to the empty glass. "I think it's time for a *real* drink."

"What do you want?" John asks.

She throws a quick glance in my direction. "I haven't decided."

Blame it on the alcohol or simply too much testosterone but I turn to Hannah. "And what about you, Hannah? What do *you* want? Can I get you something?" I raise an eyebrow. "*Anything?*"

She giggles. "I'm sure I can think of something."

185

"Come on, Lor," Sophia says as she stands up, offering a hand. "I'll help you decide." She gives me a pointed look as they leave the room.

The rest of us sit in awkward silence until John and Mason start talking about business. *Yawn.*

"How are you getting home later?" Hannah asks me, uncrossing her legs. I stare down at her bare thighs and my eyes instinctively travel upwards. I swear that I see a glimpse of her black panties. She giggles and my eyes snap back to hers. "Do you want to share a cab or something?"

Or something? "Maybe."

She opens her legs a little wider. Yes, definitely black. And lace. Fuck, I can even see the little swirly pattern on them. "Like what you see?" she whispers.

Yes, I do. I really fucking do. I just wish that she was somebody else. I look away when I sense somebody staring at me. I turn to see John smirking. I shake my head, trying to erase the image of Hannah's panties. Even though my dick is getting hard, that's the most action I'm going to get tonight.

"Are you two okay over there?" he asks, sounding smug; triumphant, even.

"Fine." I get to my feet. "Where's your bathroom?"

"Left at the top of the stairs."

I don't listen to him. Instead, I turn right. I open the bedroom door and walk in, surprised when I see some actual color on the walls instead of beige. The wall behind his bed is painted a dark red. *Interesting.* Maybe I've underestimated him. Maybe he isn't as boring in the bedroom as he is in general. Maybe that's the reason Lori's with him because let's face it, I can't think of any other fucking reasons. I walk around the room, taking in everything I see. It's minimalist, just like him. There are a few lamps, some decorative pillows and a couple of plants. I walk over to one and tug on a leaf, expecting it to be

186

plastic but of course it's real. I take back what I said about him not being terrible in bed. She's obviously with him for his thriving house plants. Meanwhile, I can't even keep a cactus alive.

I walk over to the closet and open it up. I ignore the row of boring shirts and instead look up at the box on the top shelf. Maybe whatever is kept inside of it will help me understand their relationship more. Maybe he's an undercover agent, posing as a boring dentist. Maybe the box contains his badge and gun.

Or maybe it's full of crap.

A teddy bear, some photo albums, a couple of old chess trophies and a leather-bound book. Surely it contains something important. I open it up and burst out laughing. Well, well, well…it looks like somebody has been doing some late night studying.

I flick through and stop on page twenty six – 'the peg'. Not one of my personal favorites. I turn the page and tilt my head to the side. The good old 'butter churner'. I forgot how fun that one can be. My dick is rock solid by the time I reach 'the waterfall'. I think back to the last time I tried it. The blood rush to my head gave me one of the best orgasms of my life. Of course I repaid Lori the favor afterwards. I quickly flick through the rest of the book, keeping a mental tally of all the positions we've tried. I put it back inside the box when it dawns on me that he might have done the same ones with her too. I shut the closet door and jump when I see Lori standing in the doorway.

Busted.

"What the hell are you doing in here?" she asks, folding her arms.

"I wanted to see where you sleep."

"Because that isn't creepy…"

"I wanted to see where you fuck him," I clarify.

She stands up straighter. "Please don't start." *Too late.* I sit down on the edge of his bed. "Stand up."

"Why?" I bounce up and down a couple of times. "It's comfortable. A little springy but hey, you know me, I'm not fussy."

"Stop it."

I pat the spot next to me. "Come and sit down."

"Jesus, Buzz. Will you just stop and take a look at yourself? First you snooped through his things and now you're sitting on his damn bed. This isn't fair."

"Oh, are we talking about fairness? Okay, I've got one. It's *not fair* that he gets to fuck you in this bed just because I made a little mistake. I'm only human, Lor. Don't you think you've punished me enough?"

She closes the door behind her. "A little mistake? A *little* mistake? You broke my heart."

Her words cut like a knife. "Then let me put the pieces back together. Let me heal you."

"John was there to pick up the pieces. He's *still* picking up the pieces."

"And now what? You're staying with him because you feel like you owe him something? You feel indebted? John can't heal you, Lori. It has to be me."

She begins to pace up and down. "And then what, Buzz? What happens after you heal me? How long until you go and fucking break me again?"

I stand up. "I won't. That's where you've got it all wrong. I've changed."

She stops pacing. "Well so have I."

"But *we* haven't. Whatever happens, there will always be *us*."

"Just leave, Buzz. I wasn't joking when I told you to take Hannah with you. It's so obvious she wants to sleep with you."

"I don't want her. I only want you. Do you want to know something really fucked up?"

"No."

I tell her anyway. "The thought of fucking you in his bed turns me on *so goddamn much*."

188

She throws her arms up in the air. "Oh my god, there you go again! I'm trying to have a serious conversation but all you can think about is sex. It's all one big game to you, isn't it? You just want to prove that you can have me again."

"You're wrong." I pause. "I already know that I can have you."

I should have stopped talking.

"You're such an arrogant asshole."

"I didn't mean it like that."

"Yes, you did. This all boils down to your ego. You've dragged John into some pathetic pissing contest where I'm the prize. Well do you know what, Buzz? You can't *win* me. I'm not some kind of trophy."

"I know you're not." The box containing the chess trophy flashes through my mind. "Did you know that he has a Kama Sutra stashed away up there?"

She scowls. "Just leave. Leave right now."

I chuckle. "Aww, come on, I'm just trying to lighten the mood."

"No, you're being a dick."

"If I was being a dick, I'd ask why he needs an instruction manual."

"Not everybody has fucked a thousand women a thousand different ways."

Ouch. "Does he stop mid-fuck to consult the book?"

"Do I have to drag you out of here?" she seethes.

"Have you learned any new moves to show me?"

She grabs hold of my arm in an attempt to physically remove me, but I pull her to me in one swift movement. My dick twitches when I feel her nipples harden against my chest. "Is sex with John as beige as his carpets?"

"I'm not talking to you about my sex life."

"I'll take that as a yes. Don't you miss it?"

"Miss what?"

189

"Our mind-blowing sex. I know that I do."

"Buzz…"

"Do you remember the time I covered your pussy in ice cream? Do you remember how cold it felt? How *good* it felt? Do you remember how warm my tongue was when I licked it all off?" She closes her eyes and I'm absolutely positive she's remembering how good it felt. "I'll never be able to look at ice cream in the same way again. Whenever I see it at the store or on TV, I think of you. I think of you coming in my mouth. I think about how you tasted like cookie dough."

Her eyes snap open, drunk with pure lust. "Why are you doing this?"

"Doing what? Turning you on?"

"I warned you. When you first showed up here tonight, I warned you."

"Since when do I ever listen to warnings?"

"You can't keep doing this. This is his house. This is his bedroom."

"And you're *my* girl."

She doesn't deny it.

She *can't* deny it.

We stare at each other for what feels like minutes.

And then we're kissing.

And my hands are in her hair.

And *her* hands are unbuttoning my jeans.

And then she's pushing me away. "No. We can't. Not like this." She closes her eyes, her breathing heavy. When she opens them again, her eyes are the darkest I've ever seen them. Haunted by memories. Burning with desire. If I looked close enough, I'd probably be able to see actual flames. The same flames I'll burn in when I get to hell. But I'd rather go to hell for having her than live in my own version of hell on earth for *not* having her. I lean in and that's all it takes because we're kissing again.

And her legs wrap around my waist.

190

And I'm walking backwards.

And we're on the bed.

His bed.

And she's rubbing up against *my* dick.

And I'm biting through cotton to get to her nipples.

And I'm about to fuck her.

I swear to god I'm about to fuck her right here, right now.

And the door creaks.

And…

The *door*.

"You've got to be fucking kidding me!" Sophia says, closing the door behind her. "Are you out of your fucking minds?" she whispers angrily. "John is downstairs!" She points to the floorboards. "Right there! Literally sitting right underneath you!" Lori scrambles to get off me and I instantly miss her body on mine. "If you want each other this bad then why the fuck are you not together? Why are we even here in this damn house?"

"It's not that simple," Lori replies, defensively.

"Well you're going to have to help me out here because it seems pretty simple from the outside looking in. You obviously still want each other."

"Of course I still want him," Lori snaps. "Just look at him! He's never going to magically stop being my type, is he?"

"So then it's just a physical attraction? That's all this is? Just sex?"

We both look at Lori and I hold my breath as I wait for her to answer. "Yes…no…I mean, I don't know. Maybe."

"You've just given me four answers," she replies.

"My mind is all over the place."

"Well you need to sort your shit out. How am I supposed to go downstairs and look John in the eye when I've just seen the way you were looking at another man in his bedroom?"

"Why are you making this about you?" Lori huffs. "This isn't your problem. You think that *you* feel bad? Well how do you think it makes *me* feel looking him in the eye?"

"If it made you feel *that* bad then you wouldn't be cheating on him in the first place."

"I'm not cheating on him."

"Oh, so you're just dry humping? Does Buzz suck on all of his friends' nipples?" She holds a hand up to me. "Don't you dare answer that, smartass."

"Why are you acting like this?" Lori asks Sophia, her eyes filling with tears. "You're supposed to be my best friend. You're supposed to support me."

"I'm trying, Lori. I'm really trying. But it's hard when you're turning into a person I don't recognize. We spent years trapping those cheating bastards. *Years*. And now you're turning into one of them."

"How can you even say that?"

"Because it's true. To John, you're no different to any of the cheaters we trapped."

"And to you? Am I different to you?"

"Of course you're different but your behavior is the same. That's why I'm so upset. This isn't you. You need to decide what you want. *Who* you want."

"*What* I want and *who* I want are two completely different things."

"What do you even mean by that?" Sophia asks, narrowing her eyes.

I stand up. "I know what she means. I'm the *who* but she doesn't want me. She *wants* what she has with him. She wants the security. The calm. That's the life she wants. The life she *needs*."

"Is that right?" Sophia asks her.

Lori nods, a tear falling down her cheek. "I wish that John was the only person in my head and my heart. I wish it was that straight forward. Do you really think that I *want* to have these feelings for Buzz? I would switch them off if I had the chance."

My heart breaks as I take a step closer to her. "Do you…do you really mean that?" She looks at me for a long moment and then nods. So *this* is what heartbreak feels like. I begin to back out of the room.

"Buzz…" she says. "Wait."

I can't. I can't bear to stand in front of her any longer. I can't listen to how she so desperately wants to love another man, even when she knows he isn't right for her. How she would rather settle than be with me. How even though she still has feelings for me, I'm so unworthy and so unlovable that she would choose to erase them all if she could. And the most heartbreaking thing about all of this is that however terrible I'm feeling right now, I know without a shadow of a doubt that I would never choose to erase these feelings because erasing them would mean erasing *her*.

I head for the toilet and lock the door behind me. I walk over to the sink before splashing my face with cold water. I consider what to do next and decide that the most sensible thing is to go home. I'll take a quick piss then slip out unnoticed. John would be ecstatic to hear that I was leaving and *I'd* be ecstatic to punch him in his smug face. I refuse to give Lori any more excuses as to why John is better for her than I am.

I open the door as quietly as I can and pause for a moment at the top of the stairs. I can't hear Lori or Sophia but the bedroom door is closed so they must still be inside.

I thought Soph was on my team but now I'm not so sure. I would never want to lose her as a friend, but I'll always put Lori first.

I begin to descend the stairs when John appears at the bottom of them, looking pissed. I pause when I notice that he's looking at my...dick? I'm confused and a little weirded out until I look down and see that my zipper is undone. I'm a little drunk and *a lot* hurt, and I know that what I'm about to do is wrong but it's also wrong that he gets to call Lori his girlfriend. I smirk, trying to copy the smug look on his face from earlier as I pull my zipper up, exaggerating the movement.

He looks like he hates me even more than I hate him but of course that's not possible. I purposely walk down the stairs as slowly as I can, letting him stew. By the time I've reached the bottom, I can practically see steam coming off him. "Where's Lori?" he grunts.

"I don't know," I answer honestly. "Maybe try your bedroom."

"What did you do?"

"I did what I needed to do, John."

He clenches his fists. "Stay away from her or I swear I'll..."

"You'll do what?" I ask, squaring up to him. "Throw mouthwash over me? Drill some holes into my teeth? You won't do anything and we both know it. Whoever Lori wants to be with is her decision, not ours."

"Leave my house. *Now.*"

"Don't worry, I was already leaving. There's way too much beige for my liking...except for the lovely splash of red in your bedroom, of course. What shade is that? Scarlet?" I laugh when he pushes me. "Don't start something that you can't finish, John."

His eyes are narrowed and full of hate. "I won't give her up without a fight."

"Neither will I."

"She's way too good for you. She's the most intelligent woman I've ever met except for when it comes to you. I guess we all have our downfalls."

"I already know that she's too good for me. Why do you think I'm fighting so hard for her?"

"If you really loved her, you would let her go."

"That's bullshit. Love isn't about giving up. Love is the *only* thing worth fighting for."

"I could give her a good life."

I look up when there's a noise at the top of the stairs. Lori and Sophia stop walking when they see us. Lori quickly wipes at her eyes and plasters on a fake smile even though there's really no need. "I know that you could," I reply to John. "But I could give her an extraordinary one." I nod at Lori before walking past John and straight out of the door.

CHAPTER TWENTY THREE

The water is hot.

No. *Boiling.*

My skin is red, my hands are crinkly, and my heart is hurting.

I don't know how long I've been standing in the shower, but I should probably get out because the constant stream of water has made my whole upper body numb.

I climb out and wrap a towel around my waist before going in search of my phone. I have no idea what time it is. All I know is that I left John's house around nine thirty and came straight home so that I could feel sorry for myself in peace. In other words, I ate a shit ton of peanut butter while listening to a playlist called 'Life sucks'. I decided to turn it off and take a shower when the lyrics to a song from *The Greatest Showman* hit a little too close to home. *'Run away, they say. No one will love you as you are.'* Yep, that pretty much sums up how I'm feeling right about now. Unwanted. Unworthy. Unlovable.

I find my cell and see that it's 11.56 p.m. and that I have a missed call.

Please let it be her. Please let it be her. Please let it be her.

I don't know why I'm getting my hopes up when it'll probably be Mason checking that I'm not fucking my life up even more.

But I was right to hope.

My heart leaps when I unlock the screen and see that Lori tried calling me at eleven twenty eight. Eleven *twenty eight.* Which also happened to be exactly twenty eight minutes ago. If this isn't the universe giving me a sign then I don't know what is.

I waste no time in calling her back and she wastes no time in answering it. "Lor?" I say after a few seconds. "Are you there?" More silence. "Lori?"

"I'm here."

"Are you okay?"

"Not really. You?"

196

"I feel like shit. Where are you?"

"Home."

"Is John with you?"

"No. I left his place about an hour ago."

Good. "Sorry for ruining your game night."

"It wasn't *my* game night. It was his way of pimping Hannah out to you and we both know it. He must think we're stupid."

"Nah, apparently you're the most intelligent woman he's ever met except for when it comes to me."

"He said that?"

"Yup."

She sighs. "Buzz…I'm sorry for what I said earlier."

"You don't have to be sorry. I always want you to be honest with me." *Even if the truth hurts.*

"Sophia was pushing me for answers and it all came out sounding way harsher than how I actually meant it."

"It's fine."

"No, it's not. What I said about switching my feelings off…I only said that because my life would be so much easier if I didn't feel anything for you. But the easiest option isn't always the best option. That's what I'm struggling with at the moment. I just need to be sure before making any decisions."

"I get it."

"Do you though?"

"Yes."

"I'm sure your life would be much easier without me in it, too."

"My life would be empty without you in it," I tell her. "I don't know what I did before I met you."

She laughs. "Hmmm, you don't know what you did? You *did* a lot of women."

"Did I? I can't remember it was that long ago."

197

"You can't remember their names, or you can't remember doing it?"

I chuckle. "Wait, which one are you again?"

"I don't even know who I am anymore," she replies, all joking aside now.

"You're the same wonderful person you've always been. Don't let any of this make you think otherwise."

"I'm not so sure."

"Well I am."

More silence.

"How was Sophia after I left?" I ask, changing the subject. "I never want to come between your friendship."

"She was okay. She wouldn't be so angry if she didn't care about us so much. She doesn't want either of us to get hurt. To be honest, I think she wants us to go back to being a happy family of four again."

"Don't we all?"

Don't we?

Please say that we do.

She doesn't answer for a long time and I'm about to make a joke when she finally says, "Look out of your window, Buzz."

"What?"

"Look out of your window."

I practically run over to it and stop breathing when I see her car parked outside. "I thought you were at home?"

"I am."

I swallow hard. "What...I mean, do you...do you want to come inside?"

"I've been sitting here for almost an hour."

"Fuck. I'm sorry. I was in the shower when you called. I called you back as soon as I saw it."

"It's fine. I needed some time to think." She pauses. "I got out of my car twice only to get straight back inside again. I'm not sure what I'm even doing here. I want to come in but I'm not going to."

"We could talk. *Just* talk."

"We're talking now." I hear the smile in her voice.

"Maybe when two people can't stay away from each other, they're not supposed to. I meant what I said earlier, Lor. I've changed. I wish you would believe me."

"I do believe you."

"You do?"

"Yes. But I also meant it when I said that I've changed too. I need to work through some things. I need some time alone."

"What about John?"

"I need some time *alone*," she repeats.

She's leaning her head back, looking the other way when I say, "Look out of your window, Lori."

Her head snaps to the passenger side where I'm standing in nothing but my towel. "Buzz…"

"I couldn't stay inside knowing you're right here." I try the door handle and it opens. "Can I get in?" I ask, still talking into my cell.

"Yes," she whispers into hers.

I hang up and climb inside. "Hi."

She groans. "Of course you're only wearing a towel. *Of course.*"

I chuckle. "Is there a problem?"

"Sophia would kill us if she could see us now."

"It's pitch black, I'm pretty sure *nobody* can see us now."

She lets her head fall back against the headrest. "So now what?"

"Now we talk."

"Talk or *just talk*?"

"I'll let you decide," I say with a grin.

She sighs. "When did life become so difficult?"

"Six months, three weeks anddd four days ago." She leans her head to one side as though she's trying to figure it out. "The day I let you go," I explain. She closes her eyes in response. "Do you remember when we were having a movie night and you got called in to work to trap that reality star? I think he was on Survivor."

She opens her eyes. "Yes?"

"I ended up going out for drinks with Mason."

"Yeah, I think I remember you making plans."

"Well we saw you that night."

She leans forward in her seat. "What?"

"We went to a couple of bars and you were in one of them with him. He had his arm around your waist and you were laughing at something he said. I watched you for at least twenty minutes. It felt like hours. Mason was trying to get me to leave but I couldn't look away. It was like watching a car crash."

"It was my job. You told me that you understood."

"I did...until I saw you with him." I shake my head. "You were looking at him the same way you looked at me. You were smiling at him the same way you smiled at me. Your laugh even sounded genuine and your eyes did that thing where they crinkle up in the corners. It all became real. *Too* real. Mason stopped me from going over to you. I couldn't take it. And then we were finally about to leave and you kissed him."

"*He* kissed *me*," she clarifies.

I shrug. "You kissed each other. And it lasted a little longer than I liked. I thought that once his lips touched yours, it was game over. I was waiting for you to pull away."

"I *did* pull away but I needed to make sure the photographer got the shot first or else I would have done it all for nothing. I pulled away when he tried to use his tongue."

I know she's only trying to make me feel better, but it really isn't helping. "When his hand touched your ass...I exploded. Mason had to drag me out of there. I tried to forget about it afterwards but I couldn't."

She looks like she's mentally piecing a puzzle together. "You stayed at Mason's house that night."

I nod. "I kept picturing you kissing him."

"I hardly saw you that week."

"I tried to fight it so hard but every time I kissed you, I thought about him. It was driving me insane. I needed some time to get over it before I completely ruined us for good. I didn't want to take it out on you. I didn't want to resent you."

"Time out isn't supposed to last six months, Buzz."

"I wanted to make sure that I was properly ready. I wanted to deal with my issues rather than mask them. I didn't know you'd quit trapping so I was making sure that I could definitely handle your job. I didn't want to mess you around. I'd never had a serious relationship before you, so I wasn't used to all the emotions. I started seeing a therapist and I could feel myself getting better."

"Why didn't you tell me any of this at the time?"

"I just…I just thought you'd still be there."

"You thought that I would wait for you."

"Don't you think what we had…what we *have* is worth waiting for?"

"I don't know anymore. Is it?"

"Yes, it is." I lean over and place my hand over her heart. "And in here you know that it is. I made you wait too long. I get it. Well now it's my turn to wait for you."

"I don't want you to wait," she whispers, placing her hand on top of mine. "I want you to *live*. I want to be sure that if we end up together, it's because we're absolutely positive that we want each other over anybody else."

I thread my fingers through hers. "I've never been so sure about anything in my entire life."

"You always say the right things."

"I'm just being honest. What do you want me to say? That I'm fine living without you? That it doesn't hurt my heart to see you with another man? Because I'd be lying."

She smiles. "There you go again. You sound like you're a character in a book."

I chuckle. "If this were a book, it would be one of the best slow-burn, second chance love stories out there."

She swallows hard. "*Love* story?"

"Come on, Lor. You read enough books to know what it looks like when a man is in love."

"Are you...are you saying..."

"I'm saying that I'm in love with you, Lori. I'm saying that I didn't even know what love *was* before I met you. I thought it was some stupid, airy-fairy bullshit but you've opened my eyes to a whole new world. You've opened my heart."

"Do you really mean that?"

"I wouldn't say it if I didn't mean it. There's a reason I haven't said it until now. I'm ready for this. I'm ready when you are."

She keeps her eyes fixed on mine as she unfastens her seatbelt. "I googled what I should do about you, you know."

I can't help but laugh. "Damn, Google has the answer to everything these days, huh? So what did it tell you to do?"

"Well I read a few articles then looked on a relationship advice forum. There were three popular answers. Number one was to stay away from you. Apparently the longer I'm away from you, the easier it will get. In time, I'll lose all my feelings for you."

"That's terrible advice. Did I tell you about the time Doctor Google diagnosed me with a brain tumor? All I needed was an updated contact lens prescription. You should never listen to Google. Ever."

She ignores me. "Number two was that I should fuck you out of my system."

"Okay, you should *always* listen to Google. Not the second part though. I'd rather stay *in* your system."

"Number three was to get back together."

My heart starts to race. "And what do you think about that? Did you come to a conclusion?"

She doesn't answer right away. Instead, she silently climbs over the center console and straddles me, causing her denim skirt to hitch up around her thighs. "I think," she finally says, "That we were away from each other for a long time and it didn't get any easier." My dick throbs when she pulls her t-shirt up and over her head. "I think that even though I developed feelings for somebody else, I didn't lose the ones I had for you." She reaches around and unfastens her bra, letting it drop to the floor. "I think it's safe to say that number one is out of the question."

I nod. "Number one is *so* out." My greedy eyes roam her perfect, naked skin and it takes every ounce of restraint that I have to wait for her to make the next move.

And she does.

She unwraps the towel from around my waist, takes hold of my dick and guides it right where it belongs. We both cry out as she slowly lowers herself down onto me. "No panties?" I ask with wide eyes. "Are you trying to kill me? Was that another one of Google's suggestions?"

She laughs. "I haven't been wearing any all night."

I close my eyes as she begins to rock back and forth. "It's a good fucking job I didn't know about that earlier or else Sophia would have had a much bigger shock." I lift my ass so that I fill her completely and lean forward, taking a nipple into my mouth. "So just to clarify," I say, in between sucking and biting. "Is this option two or three?"

"Both? Neither? I don't know, Buzz." I switch to the other nipple, biting down hard just how she likes it. "All I know is that…this feels…so…*fucking good*." She leans forward and kisses me. "No more questions. No more talking."

Yes, Maam. Less talking, more fucking. I'm okay with that. She squeals when I pull on a lever which makes my seat lean all the way back. We're ridiculously cramped; one of the few downsides to being six four but she should have a little more room for maneuver now. I'd much rather have her in my bed and be able to take my time, but I'll take whatever she's offering. She grabs hold of the handle attached to the roof and begins to ride me faster.

Fuck, she's so beautiful. I'd be a fool to let her go for a second time. I try to soak up everything about this moment as I don't know when the next time will be – if there even *is* a next time.

I move in time with her and when her moans get louder, I rub her clit and order her to come. She throws her head back and calls out my name - something I will never, *ever* get tired of hearing. She continues to ride the waves, milking every last drop and only when I'm sure that she's finished do I allow myself to come deep inside of her. She looks me in the eye, stripping me bare and I'm completely overwhelmed by how much I love this woman. I'm pretty sure she can see it. I just hope she gives me the opportunity to prove it.

Jesus, I point blank refuse to tear up while I'm still inside of her. "Okay, Google," I say, activating voice recognition on my phone. I pause for a beat and then say, "Remind Lori to listen to you more." She laughs and shoves me playfully.

"Alright, Buzz," Google responds. "When should I set the reminder for?"

I stroke my chin, pretending to look deep in thought. "Hmmm, set the reminder for a week from now."

"Sorry, I can only set reminders for a specific point in time. When do you want to be reminded?"

"Next Thursday at eleven twenty eight." I shrug at Lori. "You heard her - she insisted."

"Sure," Google replies. "I'll remind you next Thursday at eleven twenty eight."

"Please don't," Lori mumbles.

"Thanks, Google," I say with a grin so smug it could rival one of John's.

"I'm happy to help."

She scowls but I pull her to me and wrap my arms around her tightly. I trail kisses along her shoulder, and we stay like that for what feels like hours until she eventually sighs and climbs back into the driver's seat. I pick up her bra and t-shirt and reluctantly hand them over before covering myself up with the towel. "Do you want to come inside for a while?"

"Um, I don't think that's a good idea."

"Even after what we just did?" I chuckle. "The damage is already done, Lor."

She raises an eyebrow. "We could do a lot more *damage* than what we just did and you damn well know it." She mutters something under her breath about the time we broke her coffee table. I interrupt when she mentions the mirror.

"Hey, it wasn't my fault that the mirror wasn't attached to the wall. Come on, please stay for a while."

I want to pretend you're mine for a little while longer.

Her hand finds mine. "I still have things to deal with. I still have…"

"John," I add when she trails off.

She nods and I see the guilt shining so brightly in her eyes. I wish I could take it away. I can see how much this is haunting her. Even though what we're doing is wrong, she's still a good person. She wants to do the right thing and I respect that she isn't taking any of this lightly. This isn't some frivolous, thrill-seeking affair. This is three people caught up in a horrible situation. Two men in love with one woman. I trust her more than anyone in the world, except for Mason. And so even though I want this all to be over with and even though I want her back with me for good, I trust that she's on the right path. I just hope that the path will lead her back to me.

"Well…thanks for the booty call," I tease as I open the door.

"How does it feel now the shoe is on the other foot?" she teases back.

I climb out of the car and then bend down to look at her as I echo what she said to me no less than five minutes ago. "It feels *so fucking good*." I tap on the roof as she rolls her eyes at me. "Drive safe, twenty eight."

She throws me a sad smile right before I close the door. I stand there, wearing nothing but a towel and watch her drive away, taking my heart with her.

CHAPTER TWENTY FOUR

The next morning, I wake up to the sound of my cell vibrating on my bedside table. I reach over; expecting it to be Lori but my smile fades when I see that it's Sophia.

Uh oh.

"Good morning, cock blocker."

"Not funny, Buzz."

"Aww come on, I'm only joking."

"Well now isn't the time to joke."

Yep, she definitely knows about last night. I sigh. "Have you called to give me another lecture? I'm not pressuring her, you know. I would never do that. It was her idea to drive over here. I didn't know anything about it. I was in the shower at the time."

"Wait...what? Drive where?" Maybe she doesn't know after all. *Shit.* "Lori drove to your house? Last night? Is that where she was?"

"No..."

"Oh my god! I *knew* she was lying. I *knew* it. I mean, she was acting different given the circumstances, but I could tell that she was lying to me about something. See, this is what happens when you mess with karma. I warned you both!"

"What are you talking about?"

"None of this would have happened if she had just stayed away from you."

I sit up. "Sophia, what are you talking about?"

"She crashed her fucking car, Buzz."

My heart stops. "What? Is she okay?"

"Define okay."

"Just tell me!"

"Yes, but she's in the hospital."

"Fuck, fuck, fuck. What happened?" I jump out of bed and throw my game night outfit back on.

"Some drunken idiot ran into the road. She swerved and hit a tree. I can't believe you two. I thought it was weird how she was so far away from home."

I don't give a shit what Sophia thinks right now. All I care about it Lori. "What did she hurt?"

"She's cracked a couple of ribs and has a nasty cut above her eye. She's shaken up more than anything. Her car is a mess."

"Why the fuck am I only hearing about it now?"

"Because she asked me not to tell you and Mason thought you already knew."

"I'm heading over there now." I throw on my leather jacket and lock the front door behind me.

"Buzz, no. She's with John."

"I don't give a fuck if she's with The President. I'm going to see my girl."

"She doesn't want to see you."

"Did she tell you that?" I ask as I open the garage.

"No but like I said, she asked me not to tell you. Isn't that the same thing?"

"No, it isn't. See you later, Soph."

"Buzz, wait…"

I hang up, shove my cell into my pocket and start up the Harley.

She's in room one twenty eight.

She's wearing a blue gown and two black eyes.

My fucking heart aches.

"You didn't listen to me," I say quietly as I take a step into the room.

She looks up, a mixture of shock and relief flooding her face. "Buzz…"

"Drive safe, twenty eight. Why couldn't you just listen to me for once?" I smile as I make my way over to her. "It looks like I'll have to set another Google reminder."

"How did you know I was here? Who told you?"

"Does that really matter? I'm here now. I came as soon as I found out." I unzip my jacket. "See. Last night's clothes." She closes her eyes when I place a hand on top of hers. "Are you okay, sweetheart? I wish I could swap places with you. You should have knocked that drunken son of a bitch down. It should be him lying in here, not you."

I wheel around when I hear a toilet flushing. The door to the restroom opens and John appears, wiping his hands on a paper towel. Of course he's here. He's probably been jerking off after watching all the *real* doctors at work. His eyes drop to our hands and then back up to me. "Why are you here, Buzz?"

"The same reason you're here, probably."

There it is - that smug smile of his. "Oh, I doubt that."

Lori gives my hand a little reassuring squeeze before pulling away. She winces as she tries to sit up straighter. I reach out and steady her, feeling the weight of John's stare. "Buzz heard about my accident and was just dropping by to check on me."

"How thoughtful of him," he replies sarcastically as he lowers himself into a chair next to the bed. "Well thanks for your concern but as you can see, she's okay."

"She doesn't look okay." *Beautiful* but not okay.

"Well she's in the right hands."

"Hey," she says to me. "I'm fine, honestly. I'm just in shock. I need time to process everything."

I nod. "How long are they keeping you in here for?"

"They want to monitor me for another twenty four hours."

"Do you need me to bring you anything? Books? Trashy magazines? Grapes?"

"She doesn't need *you* to bring her anything," John says. "That's what I'm here for."

I look around. "I don't see any grapes. I don't see anything, actually."

"She hasn't asked for grapes."

"Sometimes it's about knowing what a lady wants without them having to ask, John."

"And you would know, would you?"

"I would. I *do*." I gesture to a framed certificate on the wall by the door. "Why don't you go and compare qualifications or something? See what you *could* have been."

"And why don't *you* go and fuck the nurses *or something*?" he replies.

"Please stop," Lori says.

I peel my eyes away from John and study the cut above her eye. "Why didn't you call me?"

"Why would she have called *you*?" John asks.

I'm really starting to lose my fucking patience with him now. If I knock him out, he's in the best place for it, right? "I wasn't talking to you."

"No but you were talking to *my* girlfriend. *I'm* here to take care of her. *I'm* here to get her what she needs and right now, she needs to rest. You shouldn't even be here, it's family only."

"Then you shouldn't be here either."

He chuckles and is about to reply when Lori stops him. "Thanks for checking on me, Buzz. I'll call you when I'm better."

I don't want to leave but she's already been through enough without adding any more stress. "I'm sorry you're going through this, Lor. I'm so fucking glad you're okay."

"We all are" John says, standing up. "We're incredibly lucky that it wasn't more serious. It could have been a completely different story." He pauses and a slow smile creeps across his face. "Thank god the baby is okay too."

I stop breathing as my eyes snaps to Lori's. "What's he talking about?"

A tear runs down her face. "Buzz…I had no idea…"

"The doctors and nurses have been fantastic," John continues. "They did such a thorough check on her that we got quite the surprise this morning. A *wonderful* surprise. The accident was horrible but every cloud has a silver lining, right?" He sits back down and places a hand on her stomach. "How far along did you say you were, babe? Seven weeks? Eight?"

Eight weeks?

We've only been back in contact for four.

Everything in the room blurs as darkness envelopes me.

I don't know how I'm still standing.

I don't know how my heart it still beating when it feels like I'm dying inside.

A baby?

John's baby.

"I don't know how far along I am," she says in a desperate tone. "I had no idea. I've been stressed and sometimes it affects my…" She shakes her head. "I'm in shock. I don't know how it's happened."

John laughs. "It's pretty straight forward, babe. I've put a baby inside of you."

I can't take any more.

I see red.

And then I see it running down John's face as he cries out, holding his nose.

And then I see Lori crying.

And then I'm running out of the room.

And my mind is polluted with images of the life I'll never have.

The life I've only just realized that I *want*.

The one I want with Lori.

Snatched away from me in an instant.

I make it back to the Harley and Sophia's words echo through my head as I start it up.

This is what happens when you mess with karma.

CHAPTER TWENTY FIVE

I drink.

And I smoke.

And I shout.

And I cry.

And I break things.

And I'm naked.

And I'm doing things I'll regret.

And nothing will ever be the same again.

My eyes flicker open and I pray that the last twenty four hours has just been a bad dream. No, *a nightmare*. I roll over but of course I'm not that lucky.

My world comes crashing down around me as I remember what happened in the hospital yesterday morning…and what happened in my bed last night.

I feel sick when I see Stacey's jet-black hair; a stark contrast to her paper white skin. I look past her and see an empty condom wrapper on the bedside table. Thank god for that. The news of one baby is more than enough.

"Get up," I bark.

She begins to stir. "Huh? What time is it?"

"Get up," I repeat as I push her to the edge of the bed.

"What the fuck, Buzz?" she asks, scowling at me.

"I want you out," is all I say as I walk over to my closet and pull out a pair of jogging bottoms. I step into them and when I turn back around, she's spread eagle on the middle of the bed.

"I want you *in*."

"Close your fucking legs, Stacey."

She smirks and traces little circles along her inner thigh. "You weren't saying that last night." When she realizes that I'm being serious, she gasps, feigning shock. "Oh my god, are you *actually* turning down pussy? Who are you and what have you done with Buzz?"

I pick up her dress and throw it at her. "Get dressed and leave or I'll drag you out of here."

"Aren't you at least going to make me breakfast first?"

"No."

"I'm guessing a hot shower is out of the question…"

"Correct."

She laughs. "I thought it was weird how you let me stay the night. You wouldn't even let me stay over when we were dating." She tries to imitate my voice. "No sleepovers allowed. My bed is for fucking, not cuddling."

"You have two minutes," is all I say.

"I thought you must have finally realized that you were in love with me, especially when you started crying halfway through. I must say, that's a first for me." I take hold of her arm and pull her off the bed. "What are you doing?"

214

"What does it look like I'm doing? I'm taking out the trash."

"At least let me put my goddamn clothes on first!"

"You can do it outside."

I let go when she digs her nails into my hand. "Why are you so angry? I've never seen you this bad before. What the fuck did she do to you?"

"I have no idea what you're talking about."

She chuckles. "You whispered her name when you were fucking me, Buzz. You know exactly what I'm talking about. What did *Lori* do to you?"

I take a deep breath. "Don't you dare talk about her." Hearing her name come out of Stacey's mouth sounds wrong. *Dirty.*

She looks way too happy for this time in the morning. "Hit a nerve, have I?" She steps into her dress and wiggles her hips from side to side, pulling it all the way up. "I've got to admit, I didn't think Little Miss Vanilla had it in her to affect you like this."

Without saying a word, I walk up to the front door and unlock it, pushing down on the handle. If I open my mouth right now, I'll fucking scream. I wait a few seconds for her to leave and raise my eyebrow when she doesn't.

"I need my panties," she tells me.

"I'm sure you can live without them. It'll make it easier for the next guy."

"You want to keep them, don't you? You're going to jerk off to thoughts of Lori then use them to wipe away your tears."

I can't even bear to look at her. "Where the fuck are they?" I ask, scanning the floor.

"No idea. You're the one who took them off."

This will all be over in about ten seconds, I think to myself as I walk back towards the bedroom. I'll never have to see her or talk to her ever again. I scan the room then lift the bed sheet when I can't find them anywhere.

Bingo.

I shake my head as I pick them up, massively disappointed with myself for even being in this position. Dangling off one finger and holding them as far away from my body as possible, I carry her lacy panties back out to her. "Found them," I say but come to a standstill when I look up and see Lori staring back at me.

Stacey grins, clearly loving every second of this. "I saw somebody outside and thought you must have ordered me a cab but look who it is!" She turns to Lori and places a hand on her shoulder which boils my fucking blood. "What a coincidence, we've just been talking about you."

I let the panties drop to the floor and it's as though the movement wakes Lori from a trance. I chase her out of the door. "Lori, wait!" She ignores me and carries on marching, clutching her ribs. "Lori! Please just wait a second!" She almost loses her footing. "Slow down, I don't want you to get hurt!"

She wheels around and points a finger at me. "You've already taken care of that! Stop following me! Go back inside, you have guests to *entertain!*"

"Lor, please," I take hold of her hand but she snatches it away.

216

"Don't you *dare* touch me!" I see the fire in her eyes. The disappointment. The disgust. "I thought you were trying to be a *better man*." Her use of air quotes is like a punch straight to the gut.

"I was. I am."

Her eyes fill with tears. "I think it's pretty clear who the better man is."

Just when I thought I couldn't feel any worse than I already do. "Don't leave. Let me explain."

"Explain what? How you fucked her? Go on then, Buzz. *Explain.* Give me all the gory details. Who went on top? Did you fuck her fast or slow? Did you make her come?"

"Don't do this…"

"Do what? You wanted to talk so *talk*! How many times did you fuck her? Did you talk dirty to her? Did you enjoy reminiscing about the good old days?"

"No. It wasn't like that. It meant nothing."

"Oh my god, are you really going to use that line on me? Next you'll be telling me that you thought about me while you fucked her."

I did.

"It meant nothing," I say again. "*She* means nothing."

"Yet you still chose *her* over anybody else."

"Because she was the easiest option," I answer honestly. "Because she offered it on a plate. Because I wanted an escape." I sigh. "Because I'm an idiot."

"You told me you've changed. I actually believed you." She points to where her car was parked two nights

217

ago. "We were sitting *right there* and you told me that you've changed."

"I have."

She angrily wipes at the tears running down her face. "Damn it, Buzz! You told me that you loved me!"

"I *do*."

"No you don't. You can't."

"Don't try and tell me that what I feel isn't real. What happened last night has no reflection on how I feel about you. I was going out of my fucking mind. I didn't know what to do."

"So you fucked another woman? That was your default response? Your coping mechanism? Are you going to run to Stacey every time life gets hard? Every time your *dick* gets hard?"

"Of course not. I'll never touch her again."

"You have to say that."

"I don't *have* to say anything. You're fucking pregnant with somebody else's kid, Lori! Have you forgotten that little detail? What do you want me to do? What do you want me to say? Am I supposed to congratulate you? Tell you that you're glowing?"

"Buzz…"

"Help me out here. What the fuck am I supposed to do? My options are pretty limited. Do you want me to raise the kid as my own? Do you want me to babysit while you and John go on date nights? Do you want to cut me out of your life altogether?" I want to throw up at the thought. "I feel so fucking alone right now."

"You're not alone…I…"

I hold my hand up. "Please just hear me out." I take a deep breath. "I get why you're upset. I know how you must be feeling. These past four weeks have been hell having to watch you with another man. I've lost count of the number of times I've laid awake at night thinking about you and him. It hurts, I know it does. I wish last night had never happened. I wish *yesterday* had never happened. But you've got to believe me when I say that Stacey means nothing to me. I was drunk and I thought we were over. Before you try and run away again, please try and put yourself in my shoes for a minute. The life I wanted was snatched away from me in an instant." I hold my finger and thumb an inch apart. "We came *this* close, Lori. We came so fucking close."

"Is that the life you want? Honestly?"

"If I can't have it with you then I'm not sure anymore."

"I didn't think you wanted children."

"When have I ever said that?"

She frowns. "You haven't. I just assumed you didn't want them because you don't want to get married."

"Marriage and kids is different. Just because I don't believe in marriage doesn't mean I don't believe in love and commitment and sharing my life with somebody. We all have our own vision of what our happy ever after would look like and you were in mine. You, me and a shit ton of beautiful babies. I'd love to have a family with you, Lor." I squeeze the back of my neck. "But yesterday killed that dream."

"Buzz, will you let me talk?"

"No. I need you to see where I'm coming from. I don't want you to doubt what we have."

"Buzz…"

I begin to pace up and down. "This wasn't supposed to happen."

She grabs hold of my arm. "You're the dad," she shouts.

I grab onto next doors fence as the world begins to spin. "Wait, what? What did you just say?"

"You heard." A single tear falls down her cheek. "You're going to be a father, Buzz. I came over here to tell you."

"But…how? I don't…you said you were eight weeks along."

"No. *John* said that I was eight weeks. He was in the room when I found out and I panicked. I told him that I thought I was around seven or eight weeks. I lied to him and I feel horrible about it. I knew it was yours straight away. I'm six weeks pregnant, Buzz. I worked it out with the nurse. I conceived four weeks ago but they class it as being six weeks."

My heart is beating out of my fucking chest. "Are you sure?"

"I'm sure."

"One hundred percent?"

"One hundred percent. You're the only person I slept with four weeks ago. You're the only person I've slept with in the last four weeks, period."

220

My whole body is flooded with relief. "Why didn't you tell me yesterday? Why did you let me believe it was his? Last night would never have happened if I had known the truth."

"I'd just crashed my car into a tree then found out I was pregnant. I told you, I was in shock. I'm *still* in shock. I was thinking of the best way to tell John and then you turned up. As soon as I was discharged this morning, I arranged for a rental and came straight over here." She holds up her arm, showing me her hospital wristband still intact. "I came as soon as I could."

"Why didn't you call me? Or text me?"

"I didn't want to tell you over the phone. It's huge news. I didn't know how you were going to react."

"Does John know the truth?"

"Yes. I think he always knew. I mean, we always used condoms and never had any accidents. He's not stupid. He just didn't want to believe it was yours. I think he would have gone along with the lie forever if I'd have let him."

"So that time in the kitchen…four weeks ago…was that it?"

She nods. "It must have been. The dates add up."

"I'm going to be a dad."

"Yes."

"Oh my god, I'm going to be a dad. *Me.* Fuck, this changes everything, Lor."

"Does it?"

"Of course it does. We need to get our shit together for this baby. *Our* baby. No more messing around."

"Buzz…"

"We can do this. We can get through it together."

"Buzz, I don't know. Look at everything that's happened between us in the last year. We're a disaster."

"We're only a disaster when we're not together." She glances towards the house and mumbles something about co-parenting. "Fuck co-parenting. I'm in love with you. I want to be with you. I want us to be a family. Don't you want that too?"

"I want whatever is best for the baby…"

"And what's best in your eyes? Having two homes? Teaching them that it's okay to give up?"

She throws her hands up. "I don't know, Buzz. I need some time. I haven't even been home. John is…"

"John?" I take a step back. "What the fuck has John got do with any of this?" She shrugs and looks down at her feet. "Oh my god, please don't tell me you're still with him."

"No, I ended it." *Thank fuck for that.* "But he wants to try and make things work."

"You've got to be fucking kidding me! Please tell me you're not actually considering it." When she doesn't answer, my whole body goes numb. "Lori, no. Please don't do this. At least give us a chance first."

"Calm down. I'm not deciding anything right this second. I need some time alone."

222

I'm silent for all of two seconds before the rage boils over. "Is he out of his fucking mind? You're pregnant with *my* baby."

"Yes, I'm well aware of that."

"So why is he still trying to keep us apart? It was a different fucking story yesterday when he thought it was his kid. He's being a selfish prick. He wants you no matter the cost. No matter who he hurts."

"And what's so wrong about that?"

I take both of her hands in mine. "*I* want you no matter the cost. He needs to give us the opportunity to be a family."

"And he will if I tell him that's what I want."

"So tell him." She stares at me, her lips unmoving. "Lori, tell him."

"I don't know anymore. I came here and thought I knew what I wanted but seeing Stacey…maybe I should use my head instead of my heart for once."

"No. Don't do that. Families run off love, not logic. Fuck common sense. Fuck what looks better on paper. Listen to your heart."

"Like I keep telling you, I need some time. It's a big decision."

"Fine. Take as much time as you need but please don't close the door on us. Promise me you'll think about it." I bite my lip, trying my hardest not to cry. "Promise me."

"Of course I'll think about it, Buzz."

"You promise?"

"I promise."

I wrap my arms around her. "No matter what happens, I'll always be here for you and the baby."

"I know you will." A little sob manages to escape her as she pulls away. "I should go."

"You know where I'll be."

She nods then walks over to a car parked across the street. I feel like screaming as I watch her drive away.

So that's what I do.

I don't care that I'm shirtless. I don't care that Stacey is watching. I don't care that the neighbor opposite me is getting groceries out of his car.

I fall to my knees and cry out loud. Out of fear. Out of helplessness. Out of pain.

Today should be one of the happiest days of my life but instead it's been tainted by the fact that even though I'll be gaining a child, I may be about to lose the only woman I've ever loved.

When I eventually pick myself up and walk back to the house, Stacey is leaning against the doorframe, holding a glass of orange juice. She smirks. "I must say…the juice is good, but the entertainment is even better."
"Fuck you, Stacey."
"You already did that, remember? I'm pretty sure that's why she was so upset."
"Leave," I say through clenched teeth. "Now."
"I've got to admit, at the rate you fuck women, I'm surprised it's taken you this long to knock somebody up."

"What do you mean? I got you pregnant, remember? Oh no, that's right, you *lied* about it. Get your own life together before you start commenting on other peoples." I step around her, prise her fingers from the doorframe and then slam the door in her face.

"I still need my knickers, douchebag," her muffled voice says through the door.

I collect them and screw them up into a little ball before opening the door once more. "I don't ever want to see your face again," I tell her as I drop them into the glass of orange juice and push them all the way down to the bottom.

She holds it away from her, seething, then lets it fall to the ground. I watch as it smashes into a hundred tiny pieces. Just like my heart did when Lori drove away.

CHAPTER TWENTY SIX

"Hello?" Mason answers right away.

"I need you, Brother."

He must be able to hear the devastation in my voice because he sounds nervous as he asks, "Where are you?"

"My place."

"Sit tight," he tells me. "I'm coming straight over."

Half an hour later, there's a knock at my door.

I greet Mason with the world's most mediocre smile then glance across the yard to where Lori turned my entire world upside down with just three words.

You're the dad.

"I don't know what I'm going to do," I blurt out, unable to keep my thoughts to myself any longer.

"We'll get through this," he says with such conviction that it's impossible to doubt him.

"How much do you know?"

"Everything." He looks at the ground when there's crunching beneath his feet. He lifts a shoe up and eyes the broken glass. "Have you got a dustpan?" he simply asks, knowing better than to ask what happened. "I'll clean this up."

"No. It's my mess, I'll do…" I stop talking midsentence when he moves to the side, offering a hand to Sophia who is a couple of steps behind him.

My safe zone just turned into a danger zone. "If you've come to give me a hard time then don't bother. I've already beat you to it." I turn around and walk back inside, heading straight to the couch. "I've spent all morning thinking about all of the mistakes I've made."

Sophia sits down next to me but Mason stops in the kitchen. "Dustpan?"

"Leave it, I'll do it later." I sigh when he begins to open random cupboards. "Under the sink."

Sophia leans in and hugs me. "The only reason I'm here is to support you. We love you and we're sorry that you're going through this. I can't imagine how you're feeling right now. You and Lori are my best friends. I just want you both to be happy and if that's being together then even better."

I swallow the lump in my throat. "Thanks, Soph."

She pulls away. "I mean, I hate that you went back to Stacey and I hate that Lori is hurting but Jesus, you thought the baby was John's."

I nod. "I was going out of my mind."

"I can't believe she didn't tell you at the hospital." Mason walks out of the kitchen and gestures to the dustpan before going back outside. "I want you to know that I didn't find out it was yours until after you did. Lori called me when she got home from the hospital. I would have told you otherwise. I'm done keeping secrets. Lord knows I've kept enough of them to last me a lifetime. That's why I told you where she was in the first place."

"Thanks for having my back. I know we haven't made it easy for you these past couple of weeks."

227

"I just feel like you took something good and pure and dirtied it up when you didn't even have to. You're both better than that."

She's right. I regret putting Lori in the position that I did. I should have waited until she knew what she wanted rather than cause her even more confusion and guilt. "So now what am I supposed to do?" I ask after half a minute of silence.

"What do you *want* to do?"

"I want to be with Lori. I want to be a family. I want to earn her trust back and prove to her that I'm not going to get scared and run away again."

"Then do it. Prove it to her."

"How am I supposed to do that when John won't leave her alone?"

She grabs my arm and turns it over, nodding to the tattoo on the smooth underside. "Have you forgotten about this?"

"What do you mean?"
"Read it," she says. "Out loud."
I frown. "I am the master of my fate and the captain of my soul."
"I know that you pretend not to believe in fate or anything else that could ruin your tough guy persona, but you got that tattoo for a reason." She lets my arm fall back to my side. "I think it's fate that you got that tattoo all those years ago. I think it's fate that you've got it permanently inked to your skin, right where you can see it. Without knowing it, I think you got it for this exact time in your life." I rub at the goosebumps covering my arms. "I presume you know which poem the quote is taken from."
"Invictus," I reply.

She nods. "Which translates to unconquerable. If that isn't the perfect word to describe you then I don't know what is. It's time to step up, Buzz. It's time to show Lori what kind of man you can be. What kind of man you *are*. Nobody but you has the power to determine your future. It may take some time and you may have to be a little selfless to begin with but if you want Lori, go and get her. Get our girl back."

"You're right."

"She's always right," Mason says as he walks back into the house. "Okay, I think I've got most of the glass but just be careful."

"Thanks, Brother," I reply as he returns the dustpan back where he found it. I turn to Sophia. "I really appreciate you coming over and being so supportive. My head already feels clearer."

"Glad I could be of assistance," Mason says with a wink.

Sophia rolls her eyes but gives me a reassuring smile. "You've got this, Buzz."

I glance down at my tattoo and pray that it's true what Mason said.

I pray that she's always right.

CHAPTER TWENTY SEVEN

My finger hovers over the little gold button.

When I woke up this morning, it seemed like this was a good idea but now that I'm actually here, I'm not so sure. Maybe I should wait until the wounds aren't as fresh. Maybe I'm about to add fuel to the fire. The *bonfire*.

And then just as I'm about to leave, I glance at my tattoo which is staring me in the face, urging me to honor it. I think of my conversation with Sophia yesterday. It's time to be the master of my own fate. It's time to step up and this is definitely a step in the right direction. The first step of many. I need to do this, not just for me but for everyone involved.

I take a deep breath and press the doorbell. I wait for about half a minute and just as I'm about to press it for a second time, the door swings open. John's eyes go wide in shock but quickly narrow in anger. His nose is bruised and swollen from where I hit him and all the emotions from the past few days come flooding back. "You're not welcome here," he hisses, and I can hear the hate dripping off each word.

My eyes dart to his clenched fists. "I'm not here for a fight, John."

"They why *are* you here?"

"To talk."

"I don't want to talk to you. I don't even want to look at you."

"I know that we're never going to be friends but we need to try and be civil. We need to put our differences aside."

"No we don't," he replies. "I don't want anything to do with you. I don't want to see you ever again."

"Well you might have to. It might be unavoidable."

"Oh, I'll make sure I avoid you at all costs."

"Look, I know how much you're hurting right now. If you feel even a fraction of what I feel for Lori…"

He holds a hand up. "Let me stop you right there. My girlfriend…" he stops to correct himself. "My *ex-girlfriend,* thanks to you, is pregnant with another man's baby. That's thanks to you as well. You *don't* have any idea how much I'm hurting right now." I wedge my foot in the door when he tries to close it.

"Yes, *I do.* You're forgetting that a couple of days ago, I thought the baby was yours. I've never felt pain like it."

"Well it isn't mine, is it? Now move your fucking foot."

I don't listen to him. "We need to leave all the bullshit behind us and put Lori first."

He throws the door open and takes a step outside. "I've *always* put Lori first, even when I knew that she was fucking you." He points a finger at me. "That's right, I've known all along. I don't know if you thought you were being sneaky or if you just didn't give a shit, but I knew and I loved her enough to put *her* first. Even now, I'm *still* putting her first." He shakes his head, his anger dissipating and turning into disappointment. "It's just a shame she couldn't put my feelings before yours."

"I'm sorry, John." Does it make me a horrible person for not considering his feelings until now? Or does it make me guilty of simply loving Lori too much? I meant it when I told her that I wanted her no matter the cost.

He laughs incredulously. "No you're not. Why would you be sorry? You've won."

"I've *won*? This isn't a game."

"Oh, come on. Drop the act and just be honest for once in your life. You weren't even interested in her until you found out that she was dating somebody else."

"That's not true."

"From the moment you met me, you just wanted to prove that you could take her off me. Well congratulations, you've got what you wanted."

"You're wrong. I don't have Lori."

"Good, I hope you never do. You don't deserve her."

"You're right, I don't deserve her. I'll *never* deserve her. But by god, will I love her."

He laughs and it makes him sound like a crazy person. "Love isn't enough and one day she's going to realize that." He goes to close the door but changes his mind. "Tell me something…did you get her pregnant on purpose?"

I take a step back as though his words caused a physical blow. "What? Of course not."

"You just wanted to trap her, didn't you? You wanted to trap the trapper."

"You have no fucking idea what you're talking about."

"This is all to do with your alpha bullshit. You wanted to lay claim to her so you marked her as yours the only way that you could. You knocked her up and now she will always have baggage, thanks to you."

"*Baggage?*" We're nose to nose in less than a second. "Are you referring to my child as baggage?"

"Are you going to hit me again, tough guy? You didn't break my nose on Friday so go on, have another try."

I want to. I want to *so fucking bad*. "Don't you dare talk about either of them in that way again." I begin to back away from him. "I came here to apologize but it's pretty obvious that you're not going to accept it. I'm going to leave now before I do something I regret."

"I'll never accept it," he replies. "Lori was the best thing that ever happened to me and I lost her because of you. No apology could ever make up for that."

He slams the door in my face and I take a moment to let his words sink in. He doesn't seem to understand that it's a two-way street and that I could have so easily said those same words back to him.

Except for one part.

Lori *is* and will *always be* the best thing that has ever happened to me.

I finally turn around and promise myself that I'll never look back.

CHAPTER 28

Today marks one week since Lori's accident.

It's been the longest week of my life and without a doubt one of the hardest. The hurt still hurts and I've had to stop myself from going to see her every single day. Even though I hate being away from her, I want to show her that I'm serious about making things work by giving her the time that she's asked for. I just hope that she doesn't want too much of it.

Distraction is key. I've made a huge mistake by showing Mason just how productive I can actually be at work. My inbox is empty for the first time in about three years and I've even started doing my own filing. I hope he doesn't think it's going to be a long-term thing because *fuck that*.

I've been leaving the office around seven thirty, grabbing something to eat and then going home to read. That's right, I read now. In other words, I spend my evenings staring at my Kindle screen instead of my phone or television. I'm almost finished with 'The Expectant Dad's Survival Guide' and let's just say that I'll never be able to look at or even think about a vagina in the same way ever again. I'm now an expert on crowning (women deserve an *actual* crown after that), pelvic floor exercises and nipple shields. If I was about to experience it all with anybody other than Lori then I would be scared shitless right about now. It makes me love her even more to know what she's about to go through for our little family. I've always been a fan of women, Lori in particular, but *my god*, women really are fucking amazing.

I grab my Kindle and dive in right where I left off. Ten minutes later, I'm reading about the difference between colic and reflux when my phone starts to vibrate next to me. I glance at it then do a double take when I see Lori's name flash across the screen. I jump up off the sofa but my excitement is short lived when I realize that it's the reminder that I set last week. The one which I completely forgot about.

Remind Lori to listen to you more.

I check the time.

11.28 p.m.

I sigh and run a shaky hand through my hair. I remember how beautiful she looked that night. I remember the way the streetlights danced across her face. I remember how good it felt when I told her that I loved her for the first time. I've wanted to tell her every day since then. I *will* tell her every day if she lets me.

I swipe up, dismissing the reminder but continue to stare at my phone. It's crazy how much our lives can change in the space of a week. In the space of a minute. A second.

I wish I could turn back time. I would hold her in my arms and never let go. Fuck it, one little message won't hurt. I open up a new draft and type out 'I miss you' before immediately deleting it. I type at least three more messages before finally settling on '28'. I'm about to press send when a noise distracts me. It sounds like music in the distance or maybe coming from a car. I look out of the window but can't see anything so walk over to the front door. I wouldn't usually bother to check but it's getting late and it sounds like it's coming from right outside my house. As I get closer, the music becomes clearer. It's more of a tune without lyrics.

I push down on the door handle and freeze when I see Lori standing in front of me. The music that I could hear is coming from her phone and it becomes a backing track while we stare at each other as though we're just now seeing each other for the first time. My eyes trace the contours of her face. Every beautiful laughter line. Every undeserved frown line. Lord knows I've been the cause of too many of them recently.

Fuck, I can't live without this woman for another minute.

I know without a doubt that I will never connect with anybody like this ever again. This is a once in a lifetime love. It's what people spend their whole lives chasing. It's too good to lose. *She* is too good to lose.

She finally holds up her cell. "I set an alarm too, Buzz."

I don't even know what that means for our relationship but a slow smile creeps across my face. Surely that's got to be a good sign. She taps her phone and the alarm stops. The new-found silence doesn't last long as the tension between us is deafening. The air is full of unspoken regrets, apologies and promises.

I promise to keep you safe.

I promise to earn your trust back.

I promise to love you forever.

I could have said any of those things. I *should* have said *all* of those things. But instead I go with, "Hi."

Good job, Buzz.

She smiles and when her eyes crinkle up in the corners, my stomach flutters. Fuck, did I just get *butterflies*? I thought that shit only happened in movies.

"Hi," she replies.

"How are you?"

"I've been better." My eyes fall to her stomach. "Oh, no, everything is fine," she adds quickly.

I breathe a sigh of relief. "Good. That's good." She nods and I shift from one foot to the other. Why am I so nervous? I guess it could have something to do with the fact that my whole fucking future is about to be decided. My entire world could be about to get turned upside down once again. "Do you want to…" I begin to say at the same time as Lori says, "I think we need to…"

"Sorry," I say. "You go."

"No, it's fine. Go ahead."

"I was just going to ask if you wanted to come inside."

She nods and relief rushes through me. At least she's willing to talk. I close the door behind her and watch as she walks over to the couch. *Don't fuck this up, Buzz. This is your chance.*

She spots my Kindle and I laugh as her eyes widen in surprise. "You bought a Kindle?"

"I did."

"But...why?"

I sit down next to her. "Why do you think?"

"No idea. To watch porn?"

I feign shock. "You can watch porn on that thing? Teach me."

She laughs and shakes her head. "Same old Buzz."

My smile fades and a knot forms in my stomach. "That's the thing, Lor. I'm *not* the same. I've changed, or at least, I'm changing. I know you'll probably need to see it to believe it but I'm becoming a better man. I'm becoming the man that I should have always been and that's all down to you."

She holds my gaze. "No, that's down to *you*. I can't make a person change. Only you have the power to do that."

"You haven't *made* me change but you inspire me to do better. To *be* better. Not just for myself but for the both of us." I glance down at her stomach again, even though it's way too early for her to have a bump. "For the *three* of us." Her eyes are glossy as I take her hand in mine. "And I'm truly thankful for that. You've always accepted me for who I am and allowed me to figure things out in my own time. All throughout my life, people have tried to change me. I've always been too loud or too wild or too confident. My father, my teachers, my ex's - they all tried to turn me into somebody I'm not and all it did was push me away. It made me defensive, even when I actually agreed with some of it. I didn't want to be told who I should be or how I should act. I didn't want to accept that there were parts of me that they didn't like. But not once have you ever made me feel like that. You make me feel accepted and loved and I hope you know how loved you are, Lori. You're it for me. I used to look at Mason and other couples and wonder why I've never felt anything more than a physical attraction for anybody and now I know why. Now it's crystal fucking clear. It's because none of those girls were you. I was waiting for you without even knowing it. You will always be my first and last love. Whatever happens between us, I will be the luckiest man on earth to simply have you in my life."

She wipes at the tears running down her face. "Jesus, Buzz. It's already bad enough with all of these pregnancy hormones."

I chuckle. "I'm sorry. I just want to put it all out there. I don't want any regrets."

"Well now it's my turn." I nod and swallow hard. "I know that you went to see John."

"I didn't go to start any trouble."

"I know you didn't. I heard your whole conversation."

I frown. "You heard it? How?"

"I was there."

"At his house? On Sunday?" She nods and my heart sinks. She was probably there to work things out with him. I hold my breath as I wait for her to break the news that they're back together. *To break my heart.*

"I think it was very mature of you to apologize to him. You did the right thing."

I shrug. "He didn't seem to think so."

"Give him some time. I'm sure he will eventually appreciate it."

Give him some time? I'm guessing that means I'll be seeing him again at some point in the future.

"Whatever you need," I say, looking down at my feet. I can't even bear to look at her. The pain will be written all over my fucking face.

"Buzz, look at me." I sigh and do as she says. "I was there on Sunday to collect the rest of my things." My heart begins to race. "And for closure."

"And did you get it?"

"Yes, I did. We both did. It's over. I'm just sorry it took so long. It's time for all of us to start a new chapter."

I desperately want to be a part of that chapter. I turn so that I'm facing her completely. "Look, Lor. I know it must be hard to love me. I know that it might feel like a huge risk. But I need you to know that if you take the risk, I'll spend the rest of my life proving to you that it was the right thing to do."

"John said something to you the other day which stuck in my head. He said that love isn't enough. Well he was wrong. Love *is* enough. Love will always be enough. Maybe not for him but it is for me. A couple of weeks ago you told me that if two people can't seem to stay away from each other then maybe it's because they're not supposed to. I didn't want to believe it at the time because I felt guilty, but you were right. I tried to fight it but I'm done fighting. Life is too short. At the end of it all, when we're old and grey, the only thing we will have left is love. The only thing that will matter is the people around us. I want you to be there with me, Buzz. I want you. I want us."

"Are you sure?"

"I'm sure. And for the record, you are *so* easy to love. The only thing which I found hard was trying *not* to love you."

"Yeah, please don't try to do that ever again."

She laughs. "I've missed you so much."

"I've missed you too." I take her face into my hands and kiss her softly, making up for lost time. She squeals when I gently scoop her up into my arms and carry her towards the bedroom. "Well, I guess we should go and make some babies now. Oh wait, we already did that."

She giggles. "Yep, no need for any more of *that*." She sighs, feigning disappointment. "Oh well, I guess we will just have to take the Kindle with us instead."

I wheel back around. "Oh yeah, we can't forget that."

She grins. "So you *do* love me."

I lean down so she can grab it off the table. "I do. I really fucking do." I carry her back towards the bedroom and kick open the door as I say, "I also love porn."

I lower her onto the bed and look down at my whole entire world.

It wasn't easy to get here but it was *so* worth it.

EPILOGUE
Twelve months later

"I have to admit," I say to Mason, looking around the room at hundreds of happy, smiling faces. "Out of all of your weddings, this one is definitely my favorite."

He chuckles. "*All* of my weddings? Fuck you."

"Oh, I'm sure Lori will be more than happy to oblige. Maybe we could borrow the honeymoon suite?"

He feigns shock. "Wait - you still get laid? I thought all of the fun stuff stops when you have a baby."

"Nah, man," I reply, keeping a straight face. Sure, our sex life has slowed down since the baby arrived, but it hasn't *stopped*. I'll still never admit to him that for the past five months, our bed has mostly been used for sleeping. That's if four hours of broken sleep a night can even be classed as *sleeping*. "Lori's hormones are raging. Some days I'm exhausted. We do it at least twice a day." And now we're suddenly playing two truths, one lie.

"You wish," Lori says, appearing out of nowhere. I swear she's a fucking magician or maybe I'm the magician for being able to summon her at the most inappropriate times.

"There's my little buddy," Mason says, going all gooey-eyed as she hands him the baby. "I've told you to stop leaving me alone with your daddy."

"A baby looks good on you, Brother."

He winks and lowers his voice as he says, "We're hoping to make a honeymoon baby."

Lori smiles knowingly. "You're going to make wonderful parents."

"You're on diaper duty today then," I tell him, patting him on the back. "Trust me, you'll need the practice. Just make sure he doesn't pee all over your suit." I spot Sophia in the corner of my eye, shuffling her way over to us. I have no idea how she hasn't tripped up over her long ivory dress. "Hey, cockblocker," I say to her, quiet enough so that the old lady behind her doesn't hear.

She rolls her eyes. "Not funny, Buzz. It wasn't funny the first fifty times you said it and it still isn't funny now." She gestures to the woman behind her and then gives me a pointed look as if to say, 'be on your best behavior'. "This is my grandma."

"No way! I thought you were sisters. You look way too young to be a grandma. Show me some I.D right now, young lady."

She chuckles. "Those lines don't work on me anymore, boy."

Lori bursts out laughing. "Oh, I've missed you. It's been too long, Val."

"I've missed you too, honey. I've been dying to meet the baby." She turns to Mason, arms outstretched. "Come on, hand him over." He knows what's best for him and does as he's told. "Oh my gosh," she says, stroking his ridiculously chubby cheeks. "Aren't you just the most beautiful thing I've ever seen! I could eat you up!" She glances at me and then back to the baby. "I may have to take you home with me."

"Thank you for the offer," I reply. "But I'm in a committed relationship so I'm going to have to politely decline."

Lori nudges me and Sophia sighs but Val just chuckles. "You know, you look just like your daddy. I bet you're going to be just like him when you grow up, aren't you? Your mommy is going to have her hands full."

My chest swells with pride. My mini me. *My boy.*

"Well, he *is* named after his daddy," Lori adds. "Some days I wonder if we made a mistake doing that." She winks at me and I know that there's not even an ounce of truth in what she just said. Twelve months ago, on the night that we got back together, we stayed up all night talking about anything and everything. As we watched the sunrise, I thought it was about time I told her my real name and from that moment on, she was absolutely adamant that if we had a boy, that's what we should call him. After a lot of persuasion, I agreed to it but only if I got to choose a girl's name. She was fine until I told her that she was going to be called, 'I can't date until I'm thirty five'.

"I've forgotten his name," Val says while sticking her tongue out and making silly faces. "I can't concentrate on anything other than his big gummy smile."

"Link," I tell her.

"Lincoln Junior," Lori adds. "But we call him Link most of the time."

I take her hand in mine and place a gentle kiss over the infinity tattoo on her wrist, the twin to my own. Sometimes I'm caught off guard by just how much I love her and our little family. My love for them is infinite.

"That's a beautiful name," Val replies, bringing me back down to earth.

"I guess we have my mom to thank," I joke. At first, I was worried that it was going to feel weird sharing the same name but now I absolutely love it. I feel like it has brought us even closer together and that we will always be connected. *Linked.* Besides, nobody has called me by my real name for well over ten years so adding junior to the end was a little unnecessary.

"So why do people call you Buzz?" Val asks. "What's the story behind it?"

I can't help but laugh when three pairs of eyes shoot in my direction, awaiting my response. "Um, well, a long time ago, I was having…"

"Look over there, Grandma," Sophia says, desperately trying to change the subject. "Ed's back from the bar." She points at an old man on the other side of the room. "Didn't you say that he wanted to meet the baby, too?"

"About time," she replies. "I was starting to think that he had ditched me and gone home. Who is he gossiping to now? He's worse than me."

"Who's Ed?" I ask.

"My boyfriend. We met on Tinder last year."

I laugh. "You have Tinder?"

"Not at the moment. Not until I get bored of Ed. I didn't delete my account, I just disabled it." She turns to Lori. "Do you mind if I steal Lincoln for ten minutes? I swear I'll bring him back."

"Which Lincoln?" I ask, one eyebrow raised. "Bored of Ed already?"

"Oh, sweetie, you wouldn't be able to handle me. Besides, I said ten minutes, not ten seconds."

She walks away and I'm left open mouthed as Lori, Mason and Sophia all burst into hysterics. I look around the circle at my crazy little family and can't help but join in.

I guess I deserved that.

And they all lived happily ever after.

To infinity and beyond.

The End.

<u>Best man speech</u>

Hello everyone. This is the part where I'm supposed to introduce myself but you already know who I am from the last time Mason got married.

That's right, this is the second time he's forced you into buying him a wedding gift. I had a quick look at the gift registry and you would think that he would be able to afford his own bread maker. Oh well, at least that's something that he actually *kneads*. For as long as I've known him, he's always been a dedicated *masterbaker*.

Anyway, if this speech sounds familiar, it's because I'm recycling the same one from last time. I kept it because I secretly knew it wasn't going to work out but don't worry Soph, I'm throwing it away after today.

But seriously now, in case you need me to refresh your memory, I'm Buzz, Mason's best man. And he's given me that title twice now because that's exactly what I am. I'm the best. The best dresser. The best dancer. The best driver. The list goes on. The best at telling jokes. The best public speaker. The best singer. The best in bed. ~~I'm sure some of you in here can attest to that.~~

I love Mason like a brother and I love Sophia like a sister so even though it's a little incestuous, I'm really happy for them.

You're both extremely lucky. Mason, you're lucky to be leaving here today with an intelligent, loyal and trustworthy wife, as well as me as your best friend. And Soph, well, you'll be leaving with a nice dress and a beautiful bouquet.

I read somewhere that the best man's speech should last as long as it takes the groom to make love so my toast is already long overdue. Ladies and Gentleman, will you please join me in raising a glass to the happy couple, Mr and Mrs Hunter.

Acknowledgements

To Buzz – what a wild ride! I will always have a soft spot for you.

To my family – I love you to infinity.

To Jay – thank you for designing my awesome cover.

To my beta readers – Ann, Courtney, Karen, Michelle, Rachel and Sarah. Thank you for your invaluable feedback and for believing in my words.

To Roxy - thank you for being such a good friend. Your support and encouragement mean the world to me. I'm so glad the internet brought us together.

To Colleen Hoover - thank you for being an inspiration and for supporting fellow authors. Knowing that my words have been inside your head is mind-blowing! You will always be my unicorn.

To my blogger friends - thank you for taking the time out of your busy schedules to not only read Buzz, but to shout about it too. Every single like, share and comment is very much appreciated.

And last but not least, to my readers - thank you *so* much! I couldn't do this without you. I hope you love Buzz as much as I do. Please come and say hi on social media. I read every single comment and message.

Stalk me -

facebook.com/authorkarliperrin
Search for *The Honey Trappers* on FB to join my reader
group.
goodreads.com/karliperrin
Reviews mean so much to authors, especially indies like
me.
instagram.com/karliperrinauthor

Printed in Poland
by Amazon Fulfillment
Poland Sp. z o.o., Wrocław

60539927R00150